Rebecca's Garden

____by____

J.J. Ward

J.J. Ward

(Rebecca's Garden)
Copyright © 2021 by J.J. Ward

Dedication

To my wife, for always loving and encouraging me. Without her, I would be lost. Thank you for pushing me to finish. I love you always, Ashley!

Introduction

"Rebecca's Garden" began in my mind as nothing more than an unintentional daydream while returning home from work one afternoon. From there, it grew and transformed for nearly a year into what it is today. Why such a story ever entered my mind still puzzles me, but for whatever reason, it did, and because of it, I spent the past year writing, then rewriting the tale. Though never before a writer, I have always been a daydreamer of sorts. The long rides to and from work each day have given my mind ample time to drift off into some world or other world, creating realities that were sometimes entertaining, while other times quite terrifying. Many a story I have concocted in my mind in those hours on the road, only to forget them completely as the work and worry of the day crowded them out of my thoughts. That would not be the case for "Rebecca's Garden". This story would not be crowded out, and with some encouragement from my wife, I endeavored to take the daydream stuck so vividly in my head and transfer it to paper. Little did I know when I began this process that writing could be something so demanding, as well as something so very rewarding. Though I am certain I have written with neither experience nor great talent, I hope that the readers of my creation can experience even a fraction of the enjoyment I have had in writing it.

Table of Contents

Chapter 1

Killing Victor

A solitary drop of sweat glistened atop Dan's brow, clinging to his greying hairs until it could no longer be contained. It slowly zigzagged its way through the coarse wrinkles and scars of his weathered face until silently disappearing behind the collar of his shirt. He crouched motionless behind the heavy wooden fence as he peered through the darkness towards the faintly lit residence, mumbling unintelligibly to himself as he surveyed the scene. He was much too focused to have noticed such as small thing as the little droplet. The wrinkles of his face contracted and forced another bead of sweat to begin its journey as Dan squinted his eyes and strained to see through the blackness.

Though it was cool that night, sweat increasingly raced down Dan's face and pooled around his collar, soaking it completely by the time he had crawled the 100-yards to the back of the home. It was tedious work, avoiding the multitude of security cameras, but Dan was able to take advantage of a very small blind spot on the northeast side of the property and reached the house undetected. A few minutes later, and Dan had the entire security system shut down. A great sigh of relief escaped him as he wiped the sweat from his face and made his way to the back door. The difficult part was over.

The long and eerie creak of the back door echoing down the halls of the giant house, reminded Dan of an old horror film he had once saw, and a cold chill ran through him as he stepped across the threshold. For a moment, he was lost in his imagination, but the large photo of Victor greeting him just beyond the doorway brought Dan back to reality in an instant. He stared at the image for a moment, filled with both disgust and hatred, before flicking on his flashlight and continuing down the hall and towards the basement. There, he would set up his equipment. It was there that he would uncover what he had come so far to find. All he needed was for Victor to come home.

Victor Berghoff was the owner of the sprawling estate just outside of Lexington, KY. It was vacant for most of the year, but Victor returned every spring to host a week-long party following the Kentucky Derby. Tucked away behind seemingly endless hills of swaying bluegrass, it was the perfect getaway for a busy socialite such as Victor. The secluded home was impossible to see from any roadway, and a huge wrought iron gate guarded the entrance to the ½ mile long driveway, lined on either side by beautiful white fences. Dan had been informed that he used this property to entertain some of his wealthiest…and most degenerate friends. Friends that included CEO's, Wall Street Brokers, and even high-ranking U.S. Politicians.

Degenerate indeed. Victor was a 60-year-old real estate billionaire who lived a life of luxury few have ever experienced. He was born into wealth but owing to his greed, double-dealing, and ruthless ambition, he was a billionaire by age 35. Money was simply a game to him, and a game at which he was the best. Though he loved his wealth and status, Victor's true passion was something altogether different.

It was one of sexual deviance and violence, so perverse and utterly evil that Dan became nauseated just imagining it. Victor was a known pedophile who had spent years fighting, and always defeating, accusations of some sort of sexual misconduct or another. Within the past year he had been accused of molesting an 8-year-old girl from a town not far from his Florida retreat. The details of the case appeared damning, but just like all the times before, he had eluded justice. Evidence had been thrown out and witnesses paid off, just like the numerous other times he had been charged with such crimes. The entire country was sure of his guilt, but his money and connections seemed to have made him untouchable. The law simply did not apply to people like Victor, and he knew it.

Things were to change for Victor that day. On that day, there would be no law to condemn Victor, nor would there be any to save him. He was above the law, so a justice beyond the law was necessary, and it would be Dan who provided the long overdue justice Victor so richly deserved.

Victor flew in that morning from L.A. to prepare for his guests who were to arrive later in the week. Dan peered through the large window in the foyer as Victor, with some difficulty, exited his bright red convertible. Victor's short, round body was not well suited for such a small vehicle, though it was his preferred method of transportation. The ridiculousness of such a repugnant little man squeezing himself into such a beautiful car was completely lost on Victor. His self-absorption blinded him from such things.

He seemed excited as he grabbed a bag from the passenger's seat and rushed up the stairs towards the front door. By the time he had made it to the top of the long, stone stairway, he was doubled over and gasping for air. Dan stood patiently as Victor recovered from the short run, staring coldly through the glass at the soon-to-be dead man.

Could Victor have ever imagined that he would die that day? That on that day, a man whom he had never met would be waiting for him, to deliver justice, or at least Dan's brand of justice for all his evil deeds? Victor would soon pay for his lifetime of wickedness, though little did he know the price to be paid was far more than even he himself could afford.

The past two months had been spent in planning, which for Dan, was quite nearly too long a wait. The information he received from William Beckmann, two months prior, had nearly driven him to insanity, and the wait had only added to his misery. Dan did not believe William initially, and still was not entirely convinced of his honesty, though Dan was an extremely persuasive man.

"I'll know soon enough." Dan thought as he watched Victor unlock the door.

Incapacitating Victor was simple. As he entered through the massive wooden door, 100,000V applied to the back of his neck left him lying face down on a thick Persian rug. Seconds later, he was cuffed, gagged, and violently shoved down the basement stairway where a chair borrowed from the parlor on the

3rd floor awaited him. The fall must have broken one of his ankles, as he could no longer stand on his left leg and looked to be in a considerable amount of pain. A faint smile appeared on Dan's face as he made eye contact with Victor for the first time. Seeing the pain in Victor's eyes was quite satisfying for Dan.

Victor was a short and fat little man. Disgustingly so, and were it not for his great wealth, Dan was sure he would have not a single admirer on this earth. His eyes seemed small, too small for his bloated head and protruding nose. A truly ugly man, both inside and out. Vain and arrogant even while tied to the chair. He continuously shouted unintelligible demands and threats at Dan, as he secured him to the armchair. How could anyone in such a situation believe they were in control? This was the vanity of the ultra-rich, to assume they were always in control, and for Victor, that had always been true.

He began barking orders the moment Dan removed the gag, and it amused Dan greatly to hear the defiance in his voice, as he knew it would soon be turned to total submission.

"Victor, do you know who I am."

"A fucking dead man, that's who! You don't know who you're dealin...."

Dan shoved the gag back into his mouth. Unimpressed by Victor's vulgar and unimaginative response.

"Victor, my name is Daniel Stoker. We haven't met. You do not know me, but I know you well enough. I've witnessed plenty of evil in my life, believe me, I have, but few have come close to you, Victor. I know you. I know the things you have done, and I know that you will do anything to save your pathetic life, so here is what we are going to do. I am going to remove the gag again, and you are going to tell me where your safe is located, the combination, and the entire contents inside the safe. You do this, and your day will be considerably less painful."

A scowl appeared across Victor's face. Dan wanted his money, and he was stupid enough to believe he could take it from Victor.

"Perhaps I'll give him my money, sure I could give him a little, but he won't live long enough to spend it. He'll be dead by tomorrow." Victor considered as he watched Dan pace back and forth in front of him.

The money of course was not the reason for Dan's visit. Dan was there for confirmation of William's allegations, and Victor's due punishment, not greed. Dan knew that Victor would assume he wanted money, and he would also assume it would save him. Dan expected to see the glimmer of hope form in Victor's eyes, as he realized his wealth could once again rescue him, and it gave Dan a sense of satisfaction knowing that those hopes would be crushed in a very short time. It was not simply a matter of pleasure for Dan to do such a thing. More so, a matter of duty, a matter of honoring a promise, and a matter of the unholy satisfaction he would feel from delivering justice to Victor. Victor's money meant nothing to Dan.

Apparently, Victor was not yet ready to part ways with his money, as he exploded into another profanity laden threat the moment Dan removed the gag. Dan was not surprised by this, in fact he expected it. Individuals such as Victor needed demonstration before they could accept the reality that they were no longer in control. Victor had always commanded every situation. That was precisely why he was who he was. He had always been in control.

Dan silently walked around Victor's chair, to where his hands were cuffed. Cuffing Victor had been somewhat of a chore for Dan since Victor's arms were not long enough to come together behind his back. Dan had to force them together, which left Victor in an unnatural and uncomfortable position.

As Victor continued with his idiotic threats, Dan reached forward, and with one quick movement snapped the pinky finger on his left hand. For Dan, it was greatly satisfying, while at the same time truly unsettling. Satisfying because he knew Victor deserved it, and much worse, and unsettling to know that he could derive such pleasure from another human's pain. Hearing the bone break and the pain in Victor's voice as he cried out, brought about a sensation that was as disturbing to Dan as it was stimulating. He waited silently for Victor's screams to subside, and when they did, he snapped the same finger on the right hand. This again brought about a painful scream from Victor and the contradicting feelings within Dan. Breaking the one finger would have been enough for Victor's submission, but Victor's punishment would be far worse than a couple of broken fingers if it were to adequately atone for his crimes. Dan had only just begun, and leniency was not an option for such a monster of a man.

"4-0-5-1-1. $50,000. Master Bedroom Closet." He growled his words through gritted teeth, still in considerable pain.

"Thank you, Victor."

Before leaving the basement to retrieve the contents, Dan snapped another one of Victor's fat, hairy fingers…just for fun.

Returning to the basement with the contents of the safe in one hand, and a kitchen chair in the other, Dan sat down directly in front of Victor. There was still a look of anger and defiance on his face, though not nearly as recognizable as before. Now tears were streaking down his face, and along with the look of anger, pain and more importantly fear, could be seen. He was attempting to hide the fear in his eyes, but Dan knew that look all too well. He had seen it so many times before, and Victor's attempt to conceal it was futile.

"Now uncuff me and get the fuck out of my house you pathetic little faggo…"

Dan pressed the taser to his temple and the shock from it locked Victor up mid-sentence.

"You lied to me Victor. There is only $40,000 here. Why would you lie to me? That will cost you, Victor!"

Blood began to slowly flow from the side of his mouth and pool on what Dan could only assume to be a very expensive white shirt. The surge of electricity had caused him to clench his teeth so hard that he nearly bit his tongue in two. This too amused Dan, and he laughed out loud at Victor's self-induced pain.

"You didn't think we were done did you, Victor? No, No, No…We are just getting started. Why would we quit now when we are having so much fun? We're going to spend all day together, just you and me. You're a lucky man, Victor, you really are! I know it may not seem that way now, but you truly are. Today may be the only time in your entire life where you will get exactly what you deserve. It is rare that someone such as yourself gets to experience all the pain, fear, and indignity that you have inflicted upon countless others. You will be inside the minds of your victims today. To feel first-hand what they have felt. You will get to feel it all in fullness. To see how your pain can be another's pleasure. It truly is poetic justice, Victor. Are you ready to begin?"

He mumbled something unintelligible, but no matter, he was not ready to give Dan what he wanted. It would take some work on Dan's part to extract that from Victor, as it was a secret that Victor intended to take to his grave. Dan again slowly walked to the back of the chair, and one by one snapped the bones in the remainder of Victor's fingers. Each time waiting until his wailing had ceased before moving to the next. Each time, a sense of gratification filled Dan. He could not see Victor's face from behind the chair, but the agony in his voice was proof enough that Dan was doing it well.

He wanted Victor to suffer, and to suffer immensely just as the many, many victims of his depravity suffered. After breaking a bone, Dan would grasp the finger in his hand and wring it with great force to extricate every possible ounce of pain from Victor. Again, and again Dan moved from broken finger to broken finger twisting them violently as Victor screamed.

When Victor had nearly passed out from the pain, Dan stopped and turned his attention to Victor's abnormally large ears. Overly large, and hairy, with wrinkled and sagging lobes. Before continuing, Dan paused to allow Victor time to recover. It was not proper punishment if he was not awake.

Dan took a seat in front of Victor and waited quite patiently for him to return to full consciousness. He lightly slapped him a few times to jar him awake, and Victor finally came back to reality, a reality he would have liked to have forgotten. He was still bleeding profusely from the mouth, and his hands looked and felt as though they had been smashed by bricks, yet still he was defiant. The look on his face told Dan so.

Dan sighed deeply as he stood and pulled a small folding knife from his pocket, pausing for a moment to choose which of the two thin blades to use. The clip point would do fine.

"Victor, have you still not figured it out? You are not in control anymore. I am, and I will do as I please, just as you have done to countless children throughout your life. You are here now for my pleasure, as they were for yours. You are filth, Victor, and I am here to cleanse you, and cleanse you I will. I promise."

Victor looked up at Dan, mumbling inaudible words as he looked into Dan's eyes. He had yet to be broken. Bloody and in intense pain, Victor still had defiance in his eyes.

A firm tug on Victor's ear and a quick swipe of the small blade was all it took. His left ear peeled away from his head smooth and clean. Blood spurted from Victor's head as Dan looked oddly at the piece of flesh, which did not appear to be quite as large when compared to his massive hand. Dan shook the blood from the ear before laying it in the puddle of blood that was already covering the front of Victor's shirt.

Seeing his own ear lying on his stomach was more than Victor could take. He was completely broken, begging Dan to stop. Pleading, offering anything. This was exactly what Dan had wanted. Victor belonged to him now. He sat back down in front of Victor, and looking into his eyes, he could see that all the anger, defiance, and conceit was gone. All that was left was a sobbing, little fat man who would do anything, say anything, pay any amount of money, just to make the nightmare end. He was terrified, and Dan was delighted. Their game; however, was far from over.

"Victor, we can make the pain go away. We can. But you see, I will need your help to make this happen. I am looking for something Victor. I am looking for pictures, Victor, pictures that I know you have, and pictures that I know you would do just about anything to keep secret. I want those pictures Victor, and you will give them to me, or I will cut every finger and every toe from you. I will remove your eyelids, and lips, and nose, Victor. I will torture you beyond anything you could ever imagine. I swear it, Victor. Your end will not come soon enough for you if you fail to give me what I want. Victor, I am dead inside. As dead as that little boy you left for dead in the streets of San Francisco. Do you remember that, Victor? The world hasn't forgot, Victor, but I'm sure you have. There is nothing else inside me other than this, Victor. I want nothing other than those pictures."

Dan paused for a moment before continuing. He knew Victor could choose death before revealing his secret, but Dan had to know the truth. Victor would have to know his pain would not end until Dan received what he wanted.

Dan reached inside his bag and pulled 6 pints of donated blood.

"A-Positive, correct?...Victor, I will keep you alive as long as necessary to get what I want. You will beg me for death before this is done, unless you give me what I want. Give them to me. Give them to me, and I will release you."

Victor looked up with interest. Release him? What did this guy want? More moncy?

"What do you want? What ith it? I will get you anything. Money, carths, drugths, women…juth tell me…I'll get it"

He was having a difficult time trying to speak with a tongue nearly in two pieces, and it was becoming hard for Dan to keep a straight face as he spoke. He sounded quite ridiculous, and with each word, more blood ran onto the shirt, some dripping on the floor to Victor's side.

Dan truly hated everything about the man in front of him, and seeing his pain was not something that he wanted to end quickly. Dan wanted Victor's pain to continue for hours, but he wanted those pictures more, and he wanted them that very second. Dan grabbed Victor's other ear and tugged firmly, brandishing the blade once more as he screamed at him.

"You aren't listening, Victor! Do you even use these things? I am looking for pictures, Victor. Pictures that are extremely important to me. I am looking for THE pictures, Victor. I know you have them, and I know you would do just about anything to keep them secret. I want those pictures Victor, and you will give them to me in exchange for your life. I will 'release' you if you provide me with what I demand. Fail to do so, and your future will be unimaginable. Do you understand me, Victor? Are you listening now?"

He excitedly shook his head. Of course, Victor could comply, at least for the time being. He could settle the score later. What was important at the time was for Victor to survive. Survive and he could deal with this man later. But what of his life? The future? Would what this man wanted, destroy him? He wrestled with that possibility silently as Dan looked on.

Dan decided it best to give Victor a few minutes alone to think, so he headed upstairs to explore his captive's very fine residence. It was a mansion indeed by anyone's definition. Absolutely enormous and filled with art that Dan imagined to be priceless. Paintings, Vases, and fine rugs that were so beautiful Dan was compelled to tip toed around each one for fear of damaging them. The ceilings, 15ft high, some maybe taller, were painted so wonderfully Dan caught himself staring, as if in some sort of trance for 10 minutes at a time.

"Why is it that someone so evil should possess so much beauty?" Dan thought as he made his way through the various rooms and hallways.

Dan found his way outside onto the large stone patio overlooking what seemed to be an ocean of green, speckled ever so often with the dark silhouettes of thoroughbred horses. Each one worth more than all the money Dan had earned in his lifetime. To the left, a large apple orchard stood just beyond the lawn. He could not help but marvel at the sheer beauty of this scene. It was noon and the sun was shining brightly over Victor's property. At the edge of Victor's lawn, where his perfectly manicured sod met the taller grasses of his rolling pasture was an old dogwood tree, blooming beautifully and shining bright and white in the sunlight. The tree brought with it memories of home for Dan, and a reminder of why he was there in the first place.

The dogwood tree had always been a very special tree for Dan. He grew up listening to the story of the dogwood. How Christ was crucified on a cross hewn from the dogwoods of Israel. Back then they grew straight and tall, perfect for the makings of a cross. When Jesus died, he both cursed and blessed the dogwood. He cursed it by tangling its branches and abating its size. This done to prevent anyone from ever being crucified again on a cross made from the dogwood tree. He blessed it by covering it in beautiful white blooms each spring. Blooms made of four petals resembling a cross, stained on the tips with crimson red, forever reminding us of his suffering. The center of each bloom appearing to be the crown of thorns he wore in shame, all for our sake. The people who despised, rejected, and murdered him. Even for people like Victor Berghoff and for Dan, the vilest of his creations. The story of the dogwood was a story of forgiveness and redemption, and one that had Dan held close to his heart.

Seeing the tree also reminded him of his daughter, the reason he came to visit Victor. He could picture her playing in the soft grass under the tree. Laughing as her puppy, Max, nipped at her toes. Yelling for Dan to come and play with them. She was beautiful and he loved her beyond measure. Becky was his only child, and because of Victor and those who shared his sickness she…

Victor must have been screaming at the top of his lungs. Dan heard him from the patio on the far side of the massive home. Screaming in what seemed to be excitement. Almost hysterically. He took another look at the dogwood and made his way back through the house.

"What is it Victor?" asking as he slid back down in his chair across from him.

As Victor spoke, Dan sat listening while preparing his tourniquet, looping the thin piece of rope around the short wooden dowel he had brought. Victor watched uneasily but continued speaking in a shaky voice.

"Ok, I'll give them to you, but only after I know you'll let me go. We can work out a deal. I have what you want, and you'll never find them without me."

Dan sighed again and stood as he tased him one more time in the side of the head. Victor again began crying uncontrollably, while begging Dan for mercy. He had had all he could take.

"They're in the thafe, in the thafe, go look. Hidden under the carpet between the thelthes, go look, they're there, juth pleathe thop!!"

"Ok, Victor...Ok. I'll go look, but if you are lying to me..."

Dan paused for a moment, looking intensely at Victor, then turned and headed up the stairs. It could not actually be true, could it? Did he really have them? Dan could not get to the safe fast enough to have his answer. His stomach rolled over as he rushed up the stairs and back to the large safe. If it be true, it would be more than Dan could bear.

He reopened the safe and retrieved a small manila envelope that was perfectly hidden between the shelves, just as Victor had promised. His stomach felt uneasy as he opened it and removed 5 old polaroid photographs. The edges were worn as if handled many times over. On one was a bloody fingerprint.

The images were simply too much, and Dan fell to his knees sobbing and vomiting violently. He had hoped William had lied, though he knew all along, deep down, he spoke the truth. Dan laid on the floor of that closet for some time before gathering himself and returning to Victor.

He had what he came for, and so it was time for him to release Victor. Release him from the world, anyways. He took his seat in front of Victor, as Victor sat silently, waiting for Dan to speak.

"Victor, thank you. You have given me what I wanted and so you will be released. Released from this world as you should have been many, many years ago. You were there, Victor, you were there. You stole my life, and now I will take yours. Hate does not describe how I feel for you. It is inadequate, Victor, there is no word to describe how I feel for you." Dan spoke softly as the anger inside him began welling up. He sat quietly, for several minutes, calming himself, as Victor continued to grovel like a coward for his worthless life. He was easy to ignore though as Dan had heard it all many times before.

His thoughts turned towards his daughter. The love he felt for her 19 years later had not diminished an ounce. He thought of her every day and longed to see her again, though he somehow knew that would never be. Where she was, he would never be allowed. He often wondered if she would even recognize him. Could she love him after the things he had done? After the monster he had become? Dan told himself he had done it all for her, but the truth was he was no longer sure.

Once settled, Dan inserted the gag back into Victor's mouth. Listening to him any further would only be a distraction.

He placed the tourniquet around his neck and began slowly twisting until adequate pressure was applied. Again, and again, he would release the pressure just before unconsciousness. He watched as the blood vessels in Victor's tiny little eyes burst and his lips turned a grotesque purple. The feelings of power and control and excitement were indescribable. Dan was truly enjoying himself, in a way that only someone as evil as Victor himself could. There could be no more redemption for Dan than there would be for Victor, and Dan knew it. He had become the very thing he hated so passionately.

A tear fell from Dan's eye as he thought back to all the evil things he had done. He was not the same as Victor, though he was equally ungodly. Dan closed his eyes and asked God to forgive him before finishing his task. Leaning in close, inches from Victor's face, Dan twisted the rope tight one final time and stared into his eyes as the light slowly escaped him.

Chapter 2

A Day of Regret

Having spent the last two weeks in Monterrey, Mexico, Dan was anxious to get home and see his wife and daughter again. In their 8 years of marriage, he had never been away from his wife for more than a couple of days at a time, and the two weeks of solitude was not something he easily adapted to. After 14 days of long phone conversations and staring at their pictures, he was ready to hold his girls again.

He was there consulting on the start-up of a new manufacturing facility being built just outside of Monterrey. As an engineer, he was sent there to assist in the development of the reliability program to be adopted throughout the plant. Dan was well versed in Reliability Engineering principles, but it was his ability to speak Spanish that earned him the 4-month assignment in Mexico. All members of the engineering team were qualified for this work, but only Dan spoke Spanish, and he spoke it fluently. As he laid in bed at night, missing his family, Dan lamented having ever learned the language. It was a skill he picked up in his youth almost organically. His best friend's parents spoke very little English, so throughout his childhood he picked it up, a little at a time. By the time he was in high school, Dan could converse in Spanish nearly as easily as in English. Dan and Eduardo had quite a time back then, driving their teachers crazy, speaking a language no one else in the class could understand. Sometimes while away from home, reminiscing on his high school years and the fun he had with Eduardo, helped Dan to fall asleep.

He arrived home that Saturday at 11:15am, just in time to kiss his wife goodbye, before she rushed off to work. She had been called to the hospital for an emergency of some sort. DA Langford had given a speech downtown that morning promoting some controversial legislation about whatever was the hot topic at the time. Dan could not remember much about the issue, but it had obviously roused the crowd, as three people were on their way to the ER at St. Vincent Hospital for knife wounds. Apparently, two groups with opposing viewpoints decided that a public brawl outside the court square was the proper way to settle the debate. Not long after the ambulances were called, Shelly's phone lit up and off she went.

So, it was just Dad and Becky for the rest of the day. Dan had barely crossed the threshold of the front door before Becky began pulling his arm and begging for a trip to the mall. The reason, she explained, was a matter of life and death. They were having a sale on something that she absolutely had to have, or the world would promptly end. Being that Dan did not want to cause the death of the entire planet, Becky was met with minimal resistance. Soon they were loaded up and on their way to White Oaks Mall. Dan never cared much for the mall, but Becky loved everything about it. She could spend an entire day there without spending a dime and still enjoy every minute. Although, spending some of Dad's money always made it a little better.

They spent a couple hours shopping, purchased the world saving item, then landed at the food court to catch a late lunch. They had Michael's Pizzeria pizza, pepperoni and extra cheese as always. It was the best in town and had Dan let her, Becky would have eaten an entire large pizza by herself. She sure could eat a lot for a knobby kneed little girl, and Dan often wondered where it all went. As they ate, Becky filled her dad in on all the events of the past two weeks. It was amazing how much could happen in such a short amount of time, but more amazingly, Dan would have sworn his daughter talked for a full hour before ever pausing to take a breath. She looked beautiful sitting there across from him. Her curly blonde hair up in a messy ponytail. Big brown eyes sparkling as she sat with her knees tucked inside her oversized green sweatshirt. She tapped the heels of her shoes on the seat of her chair as she spoke. Almost as if it were a necessary process to release the stored energy inside her. Failure to do so may have quite possibly led to her spontaneously exploding right before her dad's very eyes!

"Daddy, take a picture with me!" Becky grabbed her dad's arm and nearly dislocated it, she pulled so hard.

"Pleeeeeeeease Daddy!" That's all it took, and Dan was reaching for his wallet once again. At the edge of the food court a vendor had set up a photo booth that would take 4 pictures of you for a couple bucks. The booth looked tiny to Dan, but he would have tried to squeeze into a sardine can had his daughter asked him.

Well over six feet, and broad in the shoulders, Dan was an imposing figure. To Becky, he was a giant, and she never felt as safe as she did when he was near. So, Dan crammed himself inside the little booth and sat Becky in his lap. She looked tiny next to him. Dan put his arm around her waist to hold her on his knee and his forearm almost completely covered her torso.

The pictures captured a perfect view of Dan's chin and nostrils. What he thought to have been the camera lens at the top of the booth turned out to be a painted button. It didn't matter to Becky though. She didn't care if the pictures were good. Only that Daddy was there with her. On the other hand, Becky looked like she was made for a camera. Sitting up straight with a giant smile stretched across her face. She was so happy and full of life. It was easy to see that much just from those four tiny black and white photos.

Dan was thoroughly exhausted. An early flight, and hours of pacing the mall had zapped his energy. Still, he continued on, trailing a few feet behind Becky as she darted from store to store.

"Daddy, can we get Max a new toy?"

Becky had arrived at her favorite store. The pet store. Max had dozens of toys at home, but that was completely irrelevant to her. It was her duty to care for Max, and to her, that meant new toys! It was a rare occasion that Becky would leave the mall without having first purchased something for Max. Most of the time it would be the only thing she bought, as she would rather him have something new than herself.

Dan had never seen a person love a dog the way Becky loved Max, or a dog love a girl the way Max loved Becky. They were together almost always, and at night he would curl up at the foot of her bed, guarding her as she slept. He refused to leave her bed before she woke each morning. Max was a 70lb 4-year-old boxer, and he was Becky's best friend.

"Can we Daddy, Pleeeeease?"

Having not seen his little girl in two weeks must have softened Dan considerably. Those words once again produced the same result.

"Alright…pick one out, but that's all the money we are spending today, got it?"

"Got it!"

Becky sifted through the toys, inspecting each one thoroughly before moving to the next. Not just any old toy would do. It had to be the perfect toy for Max. All the ordinary toys were for the ordinary dogs. Max was special, and so deserved a special gift. She picked up a unicorn shaped squeaky toy with a long pink rope tail and studied it for a few seconds before disqualifying it.

"That's for a girl dog!"

Several more minutes passed, and although Dan was becoming somewhat impatient, he remained silent and waited for his daughter to finish her vetting process. He was ready to get home. His feet were killing him, but more importantly he needed a cigarette. He'd have to sneak it though, since Becky and Shelly still believed he had kicked the habit. And he had quit, 14 months ago, but during his last two-week stretch in Mexico, his nerves got the best of him, and he bought a pack. That's all it took. One pack and he was right back at it.

"Ok, Daddy. This is the one."

Becky had found the perfect toy, or at least perfect in her eyes. It looked kind of like a monkey, who's head was a tennis ball, and its arms and legs brown knotted rope. An ugly little thing, and well overpriced as far as Dan was concerned. However, Becky did not ask his opinion on the matter, and he did not offer to give it. She liked it, and that is all that mattered.

Dan held his daughter's hand as they left the store. She skipped along by his side as they headed back through the mall and out to the parking lot. The sudden brightness of the sun blinded them both as they stepped through the tinted exit door. Spending several hours under the soft fluorescent lights of the mall had ill prepared them for the beautiful weather outside. It was so bright, and unusually hot for a day in mid-April.

Dan was fumbling in his shirt pocket, eyes closed, trying to retrieve his sunglasses when he heard the voice of a young man behind him.

"I think you dropped this."

Finding his glasses, and regaining his composure, Dan turned to see the young man behind him. A kid, probably 20-years, maybe younger, was handing Becky her tennis ball monkey. She had dropped it in the doorway as the jolt of light blinded her. He was a nice-looking kid, slim, well dressed, with an almost arrogant smile. Dan could immediately tell he came from money, just by the way he carried himself. Smiling and continually running his fingers through his hair as he talked to Becky.

"You sure are a cute little thing, aren't you?" he said, as he leaned down and gently grabbed Becky's chin. "I bet you have all the boys chasing you!"

At that, Dan reached down and picked Becky up, putting her on his hip.

"Thanks, Buddy. Have a good one."

"Thank you, Sir. You're nice!" Becky shouted.

"You ready to go home sweetie?"

"Ok, Daddy." Becky waved to the boy as her dad turned to go.

Though he was sure he did not know the boy, he could not help but think that his face was very familiar. Dan tried to place him as he headed towards his truck, bouncing Becky against his hip as they weaved their way through the parking lot. He was not sure why, but the young man's comments rubbed him the wrong way. Something felt off about him, but Dan could not quite put his finger on it. Perhaps it was the smile. His smile seemed put-on, fake, almost as though he was hiding something behind it, and it never left his face.

As Dan sat Becky into his truck, he glanced back up to the sidewalk where the boy was standing. He hadn't moved. Still staring at Dan with that awkward looking smile. The boy waved enthusiastically at Dan when they made eye contact, as if they were good friends. Dan nodded his head and mumbled under his breath "something wrong with that one." The boy could not have been more than five and a half feet tall, maybe 140lbs, presenting no physical threat to Dan at all, nonetheless, Dan was relieved to part ways with the chap.

"Daddy, that man was nice. I like him."

"Yeah, Hun, he was pretty nice."

Dan circled the parking lot looking for the exit, all the while wondering why shopping centers tried so hard to hide the damn things. Well, it seemed so to him anyways, and he was on the verge of profanity when he finally located the exit. As he turned out onto the street, he again saw the boy. This time, climbing into a large black SUV with a weird sticker on the back. He was in a hurry and headed in the opposite direction.

"Hey daddy, remember that time at grandpa's when Max tripped you and you said a bad word?"

"Yeah, I remember. He cost me two cracked ribs that day!"

"That was funny, but don't worry Daddy, God forgave you for the bad word."

"Girl, I'm wondering how you remember it! You weren't even four years old at the time. Your memory must be lot's better than Dad's."

"I dunno, but I remember. It wasn't his fault either. You stepped on him, and he was just lying there."

Just lying there right behind Dan's feet. Max had decided to lie down right behind Dan's heels as he stood in the yard talking with his father. They had been there for several minutes discussing whether his father should plant a vegetable garden or not. He always did, but Dan thought it not good for him to exert himself so much. Randall was only 63 at the time, but thanks to a lifetime of smoking, he had but one lung, and a failing heart.

He actually heard his ribs crack as he bounced off the ground. While shifting his weight from one foot to the other, Dan took a small step back, and tripped over Max's body. He stumbled across the yard clumsily before landing rather awkwardly on his side. The pain was intense, but not nearly as intense as his anger. He could have strangled that dog, but before he was back to his feet, Becky had scooped him up with a mother's concern. She inspected him thoroughly for injury, before looking up at Dan and announcing, "It's ok Daddy. You didn't hurt him." And just that quick, Dan's anger vanished, though, the pain was not so easily displaced.

A couple miles from their home was a local gas station Dan liked to stop at in the afternoons after leaving work. It was at the intersection of HWY 84 and Caldwell Road and had been in business since before Dan's father was born. There wasn't much around besides the old station, a blinking yellow caution light, and a run-down farmhouse across the way, but Dan liked it and made it a point to get his gas there any chance he could. The little farmhouse was owned by a widow whom Dan would see occasionally sweeping off the front porch or hanging her wash out on a line.

Dan pulled into the station and asked somewhat suspiciously, "You thirsty Hun? I'm about to choke." After taking her order, he told Becky to sit tight, and he'd be right back. He was not particularly thirsty, and Becky could have easily made it a couple miles without a soda, but he needed those cigarettes. He had not been this long without one in almost 10 days, and he was starting to feel jittery.

Maybe it was the jingle of the small brass bell at the top of the door that Dan liked so much about the place. It had a familiar ring to it and took him back to his childhood. A time when you did not need security cameras and bullet proof glass and pre-paid gas. Back when a man could run a store without fear of being robbed or cheated or killed. People were just not the same as they were when Dan was a kid. He may have liked it simply because there was never anyone else in there when he stopped.

He grabbed a couple of cold sodas from the chest in the back and casually made his way to the register, stopping once or twice as he scanned the shelves for his favorite candy bar. As usual, there was no one in the store besides himself and Tabitha. She and her husband had owned the place for years, but Mark was rarely in the store. She took care of things, and she may have been the reason Dan liked it so much in the first place. An older lady with short grey hair, rather white hair, purely white. She was slim and modest and always friendly. Her big round bifocals perched on her little round nose reminded him of a schoolteacher he nearly drove crazy in his younger days.

"Hello, Tabby. How've you been?"

"Well, Hello Daniel! I haven't seen you in a while. Where you been hiding?"

"Mexico, and for far too long!"

They continued the typical "how you been's" while she rang Dan up.

"That'll be $2.50 Daniel."

He reached for his wallet and had nearly handed her the money when he remembered why he'd stopped.

"Oh, and one pack of those. There on the left."

Tabby looked at him unapprovingly as she took the cigarettes from the shelf.

"And I thought you'd quit this nasty habit, Daniel! You need to be taking care of yourself so you can see that precious little girl of yours grow up."

"I know, I know. I'm working on it, but it's just so hard."

"Pray about it, Daniel. Pray about it, and God will help you." Tabby spoke with absolute confidence as she crossed her arms and peered at Dan over the tops of her glasses.

"Good advice Tabby. I believe I will. Thanks, gotta run." Dan glanced at his watch as he headed for the door and could not believe how long he'd been in there. There was something about the way Tabby spoke. Listening to her for 15 minutes seemed like but a few moments. He would have to apologize to Becky for leaving her in the truck that long.

Dan waved to Tabby as he pushed the door open to the sound of that familiar jingle. The brightness of the sun again took him by surprise, and he threw his hand in the air to block it. He walked across the small lot looking into his own shoulder to keep the sun from his eyes. He opened the door and hopped inside before realizing Becky wasn't there. A little knot of anxiety developed instantly. Not quite worry, but nervousness. He looked behind him in the back seat. Maybe she was hiding, waiting just long enough to scare him before lunging forward. Nothing again.

He opened the door and stepped out of his truck. "Becky, where are you at? What are you doing?" He looked under his truck. When he was back to his feet, he felt a little silly. "Why would she be under my truck. She probably just went to the restroom."

Tabby's service station had bathrooms on the side of the building with entrances coming from the exterior of the building. A rare thing those days, but there were still a few stations around built like that.

"Becky, you in there?" He tapped on the door as he spoke. Nothing. He grabbed the handle and pushed the door open to see an empty restroom. It looked like it had not been used since its last cleaning. Now Dan began to worry. Not the kind of worry like a child when caught lying, or a man who is behind on his mortgage. Real worry. Torment. Where was his baby?

He rushed back into the store, pushing the door so hard he cracked the glass.

"My goodness, Dan, What on earth's the matter?"

"I can't find Becky! Did you see her? She was in the truck. I left her…it was locked. Oh God, where did she go!"

"Ok, calm down, Dan. I'm sure she's here somewhere. Have you checked the restroom?"

"Yes, I checked the damn bathroom! I've checked everywhere. She's gone Tabby!"

Tabby rushed out the door to see for herself. Dan slammed his hand on the counter, then followed.

"She's gone Tabby. She's gone. She's gone. It's my fault. It's all my fault. What have I done?"

"Check the lot behind us Dan. I'll call the police."

The police were there in 15 minutes, yet it seemed like hours to Dan. He had stood grasping the sides of his head, pulling at his hair since the beginning, praying for it all to be a dream. It had to be a dream. It could not be real. The longer Dan thought the deeper he fell into despair. He could hardly speak as the police attempted to question him. If it were not for Tabby, they would have thought him mad.

Shelly arrived just before sunset. Tabby had the good sense to call her at work. The deputies were discussing next steps with Dan and Shelly when the old widow from across the way came down and summoned the police officers. It seemed she had some information that might be of some use.

She inquired to the officers about the situation, almost as if agitated by the disturbance. When informed of the circumstances, a long, sorrowful expression formed across her face, and she began to speak.

Dan saw the woman approach the officers and made his way over to her. He stood motionless, stoic as she described the scene she witnessed. All the while, rage, not fear welling up inside Dan. Someone took his baby, and that someone would pay a terrible price. Dan would not rest until he found Becky and killed the man who took her.

"Well, I didn't think much of it at the time, but after I started seeing the police lights, I thought I might ought to tell somebody."

"That's ok ma'am. Just tell us what you know." A typical law enforcement response, but effective no less.

"I saw the big fellow over there pull in a while back. I was watering my ferns at the time. You know, if you don't water them near daily, they'll up and die on you. Anyways, I wasn't thinking of much at the moment, and I saw big boy heading into the store. Not much longer, a car pulls up next to him. On the passenger's side. A young fellow gets out and seems to be talking to somebody else in the passenger's seat. Didn't think nothing of it, so I went back to my watering. A minute or so later, I happen to look up, and the same vehicle is headed back to town. The same way he came. Again, thought nothing of it, other than the young lad was driving a bit too fast. Wouldn't have ever thought nothing about it at all if you folks hadn't shown up."

"Thank you, ma'am, this information is very important. Is there anything else? Anything at all? Could you describe the person, or perhaps the vehicle?"

"Well, it was kinda far away, but it looked like a young fellow. Well kept. Nice Vehicle. It was black, or maybe a dark blue, I can't never tell."

"A car, ma'am? Or truck?"

"It was a truck, but not really. It looked like a pickup truck, only it had cab on top of the bed. A SUV. That's what they call them, right?'"

"I think so, ma'am. Anything else?"

"Well now that you mention it, there's one other thing. What was it, now? I promised myself I wouldn't forget, but here I am."

Dan was clenching his teeth so hard his jaws ached, but if he relaxed at all he might start cursing the woman. He had an almost irresistible urge to grab the old widow and shake the information from her. She talked so slow and couldn't remember much of anything. Did she not realize his daughter was missing and this pervert could be doing God-knows-what... Maybe, if he grabbed her by the shoulders and shook, he could jar her memories loose.

"It's ok, Miss Cranton. Just do the best you can." Shelly broke the silence with a sweet, motherly voice. She too was terrified, but was holding it together much better than Dan.

"Oh, I don't know. There was something peculiar about that boy's SUV. Now what was it?" She tapped the side of her cheek as she drifted off into deep thought.

"Ahh, yes, that's what it was!" Miss Cranton pointed her finger to the sky triumphantly. "He had an interesting sticker on the back of that thing."

As Miss Cranton described the sticker on the back of the vehicle, Dan's eyes widened, and his jaw slacked.

"That fucking worm!!! I will kill him! He's a fucking dead man!!!" Dan had never been a violent man, but this was more than any man could bear. He felt as if his heart had been torn from his chest, while at the same time a rage burned white-hot. Dan was heading for his truck, hell bent on finding this man, but his wife, along with 3 deputies, managed to contain him.

"Mr. Stoker, is there something we need to know? Do you know something regarding your daughter's disappearance? Sir, calm down, calm down, tell us what you know."

Chapter 3

A Tragic Ending

Dan knew that young man. His evil smile, forever seared into Dan's mind. An image that would haunt him forever, no doubt, but he knew him from somewhere before as well. He had seen the boy before, somewhere, he knew it, he just could not place him. Where had he seen him? Why was he so familiar? All he needed to do was remember, and he would have his baby girl back.

"Remember, Dan, damn you! Becky needs you now like never before! Nothing else matters, just remember."

He paced back and forth behind Shelly as she spoke with the officers. They were calling in an All- Points- Bulletin for the boy and vehicle. Every law enforcement officer in the state would soon be searching for Becky.

"The boy is local. I know he is. He's somewhere in the city. Now go find him and bring my daughter back!"

"Mr. Stoker, what makes you say that?"

"I know him. I mean, I've seen him before. Not just earlier today, but somewhere else. He's in the city, I know he's in the city. Find my baby! Please...find her..." Dan's voice faded away as he continued to pace and think. He knew the boy, and he knew he had to remember.

"Mr. Stoker, we are doing everything we can. Please, go home and we will notify you as soon as we have more information." Deputy Johnson gently placed his hand on Dan's shoulder and walked with him to his truck. "I promise you sir. The moment we have any new information, I will let you know. Now get some rest and we will talk in the morning."

Dan wiped the tears from his face before climbing into the driver's seat. He gripped the steering wheel with all his might as he thought back to earlier in the day, how happy Becky was then, and how terrified she must be now. Gripping it so hard his hands turned white, and the leather on the wheel strained to stay together. He pulled the pack of cigarettes from his pocket and threw them in the floor, almost as if blaming them for the kidnapping. He glanced down at them and noticed the pictures. In Becky's seat lay the four little black and white pictures taken earlier. At the sight of her beaming smile, Dan again broke down. Uncontrollably shaking, sobbing, regretting, blaming, raging. Emotions completely draining the energy and life from Dan. He could not understand why, but he was sleepier than he had ever been in his entire life. He could have laid his head there on the steering wheel and slept through the night. He would of course not sleep that night though, he had to keep going.

He told the officers and Shelly he was going home, but that was a lie. How could he? He had to find Becky. The key to finding her was trapped inside his head. He had to remember, and there was no time for sleep. The city wasn't that big, and the boy's vehicle would be so easy to spot. If he found him before the police did…well then…there would be no need for police. He had to keep looking and keep thinking.

Maybe a drive through town would jar his memory. A street sign, a neighborhood, a storefront, anything might trigger his memory. He started at the mall. Right where he had met the boy. The lot looked so different at that time of night. Empty and dark, precisely the way Dan felt at that moment. Looking up into the night sky he called out, "Help me, Father…Help my baby."

It seemed as though the prayer had been answered in that very moment. With his eyes still focused on the star speckled sky Dan whispered, "Cameras."

That was it. Surveillance cameras at the mall would have something. Why hadn't anyone thought of that sooner? He fumbled for his phone inside his front pocket and excitedly called Deputy Johnson. There was a camera on one of the light poles in the parking lot, aimed right where the boy had parked. It must have caught something that would help. A clear picture of the boy, or even better, the license plate number.

"Thank you, Mr. Stoker but we already have a deputy reviewing all the footage captured at the mall. I know you want to help, but trust me, we are on it, and we will find your daughter. We are looking at all surveillance taken in the area, not just the mall. You have to try and get some rest, sir, and let us do our jobs." Deputy Johnson sighed as he hung up the phone.

Somewhat relieved, but not satisfied, Dan hung up and continued his search. He drove throughout the night. Throughout the city, everywhere. Through neighborhood after neighborhood, subdivision after subdivision. He even jumped the fence to a couple of gated communities, hoping to spot the boy's vehicle. He was nowhere to be found, though Dan knew he was close.

As the sun came up, Dan was pulling into his driveway. Shelly was already moving about the house when his headlights lit up the garage door. As a matter of fact, she had not slept at all either. She looked old in the morning light as she met Dan at the door. A night of that type of worry would age anyone. They were both so tired they could barely speak, but neither wanted to stop to rest. He spent the night searching the city, she spent the night searching for God. She prayed almost without stopping. Crying until she simply could not anymore. She felt like a shadow, like most of her was gone. Nothing left but the blackness of despair and pain.

They sat on the sofa together, silently. The quiet only broken occasionally by the muffled sounds of Shelly's sobs. Without looking at her, Dan took her hand in his and gently squeezed. It made them both feel better, or perhaps…just less bad. They sat in silence for nearly an hour before Dan stood.

"I'm going to take a shower. Then head back out."

Shelly did not speak, just a quick nod of approval before returning to her blank stare across the room. She seemed better last night, but as more time had passed, her worry grew. Her imagination took control of her, and the thoughts that were entering her mind were too much for her. What was that man doing with her baby?

When Dan returned from the shower, Shelly was asleep, sitting on the sofa with her head in one hand. He did not blame her. He laid her down across the sofa and covered her with a small, checkered blanket she had made for him years back. He made a cup of coffee before leaving, almost out of habit, and called Max to come.

The pair rode side-by-side towards town. Dan, with his right arm resting on Max's back, scratching him on the head the whole way.

"Max would kill this man, no doubt, if he knew what he'd done. We're going to find him, Max, and when we do..." Dan was trying hard to keep his mind away from the bad thoughts. The thoughts of what was being done to his Becky. Thoughts of her pain, or terror, or sorrow or abandonment or hopelessness. The only thing keeping his mind from thoughts such as those was to think of the price the boy would pay. And he would pay if Dan had anything to do with it. Thinking about Becky was too painful. He could only think of the boy.

Dan and Max spent the next 10 hours driving the city. Never stopping, always looking. At times Dan seemed to hallucinate. He saw the truck, then it was gone. The boy walking along the street. He turned the corner, and then vanished. He had been awake for over 36 hours when his blinks turned into sleep. He fought it for as long as he could. A blink, then he would wake in the other lane, or in the grass, over and over again, until finally he did not wake. That is, not until Deputy Johnson was cutting his seatbelt and attempting to pull him from his truck. He was at the bottom of an embankment, bloody and confused. He had fallen asleep and drifted off the highway, only to be stopped by a large hickory tree in the fence line at the bottom of the hill.

Max was barking from outside the truck, making Dan's head hurt even worse. He'd never had such a terrible headache before, and after seeing the blood running down his face through his rearview mirror, he knew exactly why.

"Mr. Stoker, are you ok? Let's get you out of there."

Dan turned to Deputy Johnson and threw his arm around the officer's neck as he helped Dan from the vehicle. Behind Deputy Johnson stood Max, wagging his nub violently as he continued to bark at Dan. He appeared unharmed from the violent collision with the old tree.

"How is it that Max is without a scratch, and I look I've been mauled by a brown bear?" Dan thought to himself.

"I'm fine, I guess."

"I thought I told you to stay home, Mr. Stoker. By the looks of that knot and gash on your head, you're going to get to stay at St. Vincent instead. Maybe tomorrow too. You're going to need some stitches for sure. Just sit down here, I've got an ambulance on the way."

He must have passed out, and for some time, for when Dan awoke, he was in a hospital bed at St. Vincent, and it was Monday morning. He sat up and peered around the cold, gray room. His mind was foggy, and his head hurt terribly, and for just a moment he had forgotten what happened Saturday. The moment passed quickly and at the remembrance of the incident, Dan vomited on the floor beside the bed. Throwing the sheets from his body, he tried to stand, but was met by two nurses who had rushed in the room. Dan was very weak and dizzy, and after a brief attempt to throw off the nurses, he was back in bed and properly sedated.

"I have to find Becky. I have to find her...I have to..."

"We know Mr. Stoker, we know, trust us honey, but you aren't in any condition to go anywhere. We've got to take care of you first, Ok. We have to run a few more test to make sure you're ok. Try to relax and we'll have you out of here before you know it."

Dan did not respond. He was in and out of consciousness. Thinking of Becky, then dreaming, then back again, in limbo between two worlds. He remained at St. Vincent until Tuesday morning when he was released, with strict instructions from the doctors to take his medications on-time and to refrain from driving for the next few days. Still very groggy from the medications, Dan was wheeled out to the parking lot where Shelly was waiting in her car.

She looked terrible. Just pitiful, and it hurt Dan that he could not help her. She was not crying as he was helped into the car, although it was obvious, she had been. His wife looked as though she had lost 20lbs from her already slender frame. They drove in absolute silence for the entire ride home. Both too consumed by their thoughts to speak.

Deputy Johnson and another officer were waiting on the Stoker's front porch, hats in hand as the two pulled in the driveway. Dan tried to make himself believe they had good news, but the long sorrowful expressions on their faces told him otherwise. Their eyes were filled with tears as Deputy Johnson began to speak. His voice cracked on his first attempt, and he cleared his throat and wiped his eyes before trying again.

"Mr. and Mrs. Stoker, I'm afraid we have some terrible news. Uhh Hummm." He cleared his throat once again to hold back his tears. His heart was so heavy he could hardly breathe. Deputy Johnson was clearly and genuinely upset, but he knew the pain the Stoker's would be shouldering was far, far greater. "We, um...we...we've found Becky, Mr. and Mrs. Stoker...we found her body this morning just outside of town. I'm so sorry...I truly am."

Dan let out a muffled sob at the words. Shelly stood motionless, staring blankly at the Deputy before dropping to the ground. Deputy Johnson caught her as she fell and sat her in the chair on the front porch. She did not speak, as streams of tears ran silently down her face soaking the collar of her shirt. Dan had to grab the railing on the porch to keep from falling himself. Grief and pain could not describe the moment, and at that moment, Dan too died. There was no love left in him. And Shelly was no more than a ghost.

The deputies had to carry Shelly to the squad car. Dan followed behind staggering from both, the medication, and his new reality. They had Becky at the county morgue and the Stokers would have to identify their baby's body. No parent should have to endure such a thing. No one.

The scene at the morgue was ineffable. As the group made their way down the hallway, a fluorescent light above them flickered on and off giving the long shadowy corridor an eerie feeling. Dan paused at the heavy swinging doors at the entrance to the room where Becky lay. A tear hit the floor as Deputy

Johnson placed his hand on Dan's shoulder. No words were said. Deputy Johnson waited as Dan mustered the courage to look at his baby girl. He pushed the door open and made for the stainless-steel table in the corner of the room. The medical examiner stood unmoving as he approached. The Deputies were behind Dan, both grasping Shelly under an arm to keep her on her feet.

It was Becky. Dan's soul was crushed at her sight, and would it have done any good, he would have killed everyone around him at that moment, just to bring her back. He would have died to bring her back. He looked up and nodded to Deputy Johnson, then turned back to Becky.

"I'm so sorry, baby. This is Daddy's fault. I'm so sorry...forgive me..." He kissed her on her forehead as more tears ran from his face, and now onto hers.

Shelly took one glance at the table and turned her back. She could not look at what was left of her beautiful baby girl. It wasn't her, just an empty shell. The deputies helped Shelly to a chair in the corner where she sat and sobbed while Dan continued.

Dan studied the smoky, gray, dead eyes of his daughter. The cuts and bruises across her body. Her broken and dislocated fingers. He took it all in, all the horror. Her lips were purple and split open. And around her neck was a thin purplish bruise. He could tell it was from a thin piece of rope. His baby girl had been strangled.

Dan listened as the medical examiner described cause of death. He could see in his mind, quite vividly, that little wretch, as he beat, and tortured, and raped his baby. He could see the enjoyment on his face, and the horror in Becky's eyes. He knew what the boy had done, and he could feel the pain and torment Becky must have endured. Rage like he had never felt before burned inside Dan, and he lost all self- control. He pounded his fists on an empty steel table to his side, so hard and for so long, it nearly folded in on itself. He cursed and screamed so violently the veins in his neck bulged and moved, as if they were alive under his skin. He crossed the room destroying everything in his path, scaring the medical examiner into the next room, and forcing the deputies to draw their tasers.

Shelly never moved, or even acknowledged his violence. She sat staring at the wall. The deputies on the other hand were duty bound to stop Dan. They understood his anger but could not let him continue. Deputy Johnson approached Dan cautiously from behind and hit him with his taser on the back of the neck. This dropped Dan instantly and stunned him just long enough for Deputy Johnson to cuff him. He had no intention of arresting Dan, but he had to control him long enough to calm him down. He helped Dan back to his feet, and Dan stood, staring at nothing, and breathing like a rampaging bull.

"Damn it, Dan! You've got to settle yourself down! You don't want to go to jail today. You've got more important things to do, like taking care of Shelly. Look at her, Dan! She needs you."

Dan looked coldly at Shelly, then back to Deputy Johnson.

"You better find him. I find him? There's gonna be another body in here. I swear it. I will kill him. I'd kill him 100 times over if I could, and I'd enjoy every bit of it. I want his blood."

"Take it easy, Dan."

"I swear it. I swear to God Almighty, I will find him, and I will make him pay."

Shelly scoffed at his comments. Everything Dan was doing, everything he was saying was utterly pointless in her eyes. He sounded like a fool.

Deputy Johnson escorted Dan from the building, still cuffed, while the other officer helped Shelly back into the squad car.

"Now if I take these things off, you gonna behave?"

Dan nodded, though not entirely sure he could do so. He sat in the back seat rubbing his wrists as the deputies pulled out onto the highway.

The county morgue was on the other side of the city, an area Dan rarely visited. He'd been down this road Saturday night, but it looked completely different during the day. Trees lined the sides of the roads and were divided regularly by various advertisements on billboards. Some old, half hidden by the overgrown trees around them.

He stared out the window unexcitedly, as the billboards passed in and out of view like fenceposts. So many of them years old, as if companies had completely abandoned that type of advertisement. Maybe the internet had made the old billboards obsolete.

Deputy Johnson was stopped at a red light when Dan noticed it. A billboard off to the left, half hidden from the overgrowth around it. It looked familiar to Dan. It was a political ad from 4yrs prior, when District Attorney Langford was running for election. He vaguely remembered the ad because it was one of those cheesy political ads where the candidate poses with the happy family to appear squeaky clean to all the voters. Great big fake smiles on everyone's faces, dressed immaculately. They wanted to look like the family that all families wanted to be.

Deputy Johnson had made it halfway through the intersection when Dan bellowed, "stop the fucking car!! Stop it now, stop, stop, stop!!"

"What in the hell are you talking about, Dan? I'm not stopping in the middle of an intersection. What's going on?"

"Stop the car Johnson or I swear I will destroy this car from the inside out. Do it now!"

Deputy Johnson hesitantly pulled to the side of the road and stopped.

"You gonna tell me what's going on, Dan?"

"Just let me out of the car. I have to see something."

"If I let you out, you better not make me regret it." Johnson turned and looked Dan in the eye authoritatively.

"I won't. Now let me out."

Deputy Johnson opened the door, and Dan walked across the roadway towards the billboard, without any regard to the passing cars. He continued until he was directly in front of the old sign. Close enough so the overgrown trees were no longer blocking his view. There was DA Langford, suit, and tie, next to his lovely young wife, both smiling just a little too much to be believable. Sitting in between the two, with their hands on either shoulder was the boy. Maybe 15 or 16 at the time, but it was most definitely him. He had the same stylish hair and the same phony smile.

"What the heck, Dan? You trying to get yourself killed? Look, I can't imagine what you are going through right now, but you've got to..."

"That's him. That's the boy."

"Who's, Who?" Deputy Johnson turned around looking in all directions, but no one was around them.

"Up there, that's the boy." Dan's voice was low and calm at that point. He raised his arm and pointed to the billboard above them. "That is him. Now go get him. Take me to him."

"Marvin Langford? Dan, have you lost your mind?"

"Not him...the boy. I knew I'd seen him before. Had I remembered earlier, we could have saved Becky...She'd still be here...this is my fault." Dan dropped his head in shame.

Deputy Johnson was already on the radio with dispatch.

"Dan, we're sending someone to his place right now to check it out. Come on, I'll take you home and head over there myself."

Dan obliged and made his way back to the cruiser. Perhaps it was better he did not see that boy, for if he had the opportunity, he would snap his neck. He couldn't go to prison and leave Shelly. She needed him. She was a total mess, and she would need him even more in the coming days.

"Just get him, Johnson. Get him before I have a chance." He looked over at Shelly, who seemed to be completely oblivious to everything. She was staring intently at the head rest in front of her as if it was absolutely fascinating her. Dan took her by the hand, but she remained unchanged. She never took her eyes off the head rest, never said a word, never moved a muscle, for the entire ride home.

"She's in shock." Dan thought to himself as he looked at her frail little slumping figure. He had to be strong now. For Shelly.

Deputy Johnson sped down the highway, with lights and sirens blaring. Driving faster than Dan had ever experienced. He held Shelly's hand and tried not to look at the road. The white hashes were blurring together, and it was making his head hurt even worse.

When they pulled into the drive, Deputy Johnson and his partner jumped out and helped Shelly to the door. They were rushing but still very gentle. Dan looked at Deputy Johnson and thanked him before unlocking the door and stepping inside.

"We're going to get him, Mr. and Mrs. Stoker. Don't worry."

Dan nodded; Shelly did not even acknowledge the pledge. Dan shut the door behind them and followed Shelly down the hall towards the bedroom. She stopped at the doorway and turned to Dan.

"You know Daniel…what you said at the morgue was right. This is all your fault." She said as she reached into her pocket and removed the pack of cigarettes that were found in Dan's truck after his accident. "You're gonna need these." She shut the door behind her and locked it.

Dan was overwhelmed with shame. He knew his wife was right. It was his fault, and he would have to live with that fact for the rest of his life. He turned and walked back down the hall to the living room sofa and sat down. He could not get the image of Becky lying on that table out of his head. Her dead eyes were haunting him as he sat there in silence.

Moments later, a loud pop came from the other end of the house. Dan's stomach turned upside down, for he knew that it was a gunshot.

"No, no, no, no, no, no, no…" he repeated as he charged down the hallway and through the locked bedroom door. Lying on the edge of the bed in a puddle of her blood was Shelly. She had taken her own life. The pain of losing Becky was simply too much for her to bear.

Dan grabbed the phone and called 9-1-1. After a quick and panicked conversation with the operator, he dropped it and fell at Shelly's side. She was already gone. He knew it by the same dead eyes that he saw in Becky earlier in the day. A single shot and all that was left of his family had been erased. The boy had taken everything from him. Dan sat in the floor by her side weeping until the paramedics arrived.

Dan would bury both his girls by week's end.

Chapter 4
Falling Apart

Mason Langford was the adopted stepson of District Attorney Marvin Langford. Mason was 3yrs old when Marvin and his mother, Elaine, had married, and Marvin legally adopted Mason when he was 8. Elaine had given birth to Mason when she was only 18, the result of a teenager's idea of true love. A romance that ended with the father leaving for college and abandoning Elaine and Mason.

Marvin was 6yrs the elder of Elaine. He had just finished Law school when the two met at a coffee shop in the city. Elaine was a 20yr old college student at the time. They both came from wealthy families and took a liking to one another almost instantly. After dating for a year, they married with an extravagant wedding on Lake Pontes.

Marvin took to Mason early on. He treated him as his own, always looking for ways the two could bond. The pair would spend a week at Lake Pontes at minimum twice per year. A couple of years, when Mason was in his early teens, they spent 4 weeks there. Just the two of them, camping and fishing and enjoying themselves thoroughly.

Mason's problems started in high school. His temper and false sense of entitlement seemed to be the source of most of his issues, but the drugs were what got him in the most trouble. Perhaps it was the kids he chose to be around, or maybe there was simply something rotten inside Mason all along. Either way, he persisted in his unsavory ways until he was expelled from his private school. At 18yrs of age, Mason could no longer be controlled, or tolerated by the Langfords, and they moved him out of their home.

He wasn't kicked to the curb though. That is not how the rich handle their difficult relatives, especially the rich with political aspirations. Marvin purchased a large apartment for Mason in the city, and furnished him with a monthly stipend, provided that Mason not embarrass the family. The situation seemed agreeable to all involved, and so Mason and Marvin parted ways. The two hadn't spoken in over two years at the time of Becky's abduction.

Though he never changed his ways, Mason managed to stay out of the spotlight for those two years. He was a drug addict and sexual deviant, but he was also discreet. No one knew just how evil the young man had become, and his mother and stepfather were absolutely leveled by the reports of his kidnapping and murder of Becky Stoker. Marvin and Elaine heard the news first via police scanner as Deputy Johnson called in the request. Immediately followed by dozens of phone calls from people all over city. How could he have done such a thing? They knew he had problems, but this? Could he be that evil?

Police SRT was on scene in less than thirty minutes. Arriving at Mason's apartment complex in their armored vehicle and armed as if going to war. They exited the vehicle with speed and hastily, one by one headed up the staircase. They did not bother with a knock at the door. A swift lunge with the battering ram and the team entered the apartment with tactical precision, clearing each room as they went.

The scene inside Mason's bedroom looked almost identical to the scene Dan was simultaneously experiencing in his own bedroom. Mason lying on his side at the edge of the bed. One bullet wound to the side of his skull, and a puddle of dried blood beneath him. He had taken his own life. It appeared he had done so sometime late Monday or possibly in the early hours of Tuesday morning.

Mason was evil without a doubt but not stupid. He must have known he would be caught. There were cameras everywhere, and yet he could not control himself when he laid his eyes on Becky. He had to have her, even at the cost of his own life. Perhaps the consequences never entered his mind. He saw something he wanted, and he was entitled to have it. Either way, he was dead, and with him any chance of justice for Becky.

DA Langford held a press conference that afternoon and delivered a tearful apology to the Stoker family and offered his condolences. His expressions of sympathy and guilt were sincere and listening to his words seemed to comfort Dan. Marvin spoke of Mason's past problems and how he should have seen the signs and gotten Mason the help he needed. He was a troubled young man with a diseased mind, and instead of helping him, Marvin had swept him under the rug and out of his life.

Privately, Marvin offered to take care of the funeral arrangements for both, Becky and Shelly. Dan accepted, as he was not mentally fit to arrange for anything. He also booked Dan a hotel room and rental car indefinitely, putting all expenses on his personal credit card. It was well that he did so, as Dan could not bear to go back to his house.

The funerals for Dan's girls were held as one, that Friday, and his entire life was laid to rest, side-by-side at the edge of Sycamore Grove Cemetery. It was cooler than normal, and a steady rain persisted as Dan stood and said his final goodbyes. The cold drops of rain mixed with his tears as they ran down his face. He was soaked to the bone and as tired as a man could be.

> "Our Father, who art in heaven,
> hallowed be thy Name,
> thy kingdom come,
> thy will be done,
> on earth as it is in heaven.
>
> Give us this day our daily bread.
> And forgive us our trespasses,
> as we forgive those
> who trespass against us.
>
> And lead us not into temptation,
> but deliver us from evil.

For thine is the kingdom,
and the power, and the glory,
for ever and ever. Amen."

The words of the Reverend's closing prayer were very hard for Dan. How could he forgive? He knew that God was the Creator of life…of everything. Holy and Righteous. That he was to follow the commandments set forth by Him, but knowing he should, and being able to do so, were entirely separate things. And of all the feelings and desires swirling around inside his head, forgiveness was not one.

Sleep, however, was. He had not slept more than a few hours total in the past 7 days, and it showed. He could not focus his mind on anything, and his words were frustratingly being lost as he tried to speak. His appearance was no better. Unshaven for a week with large dark bags under his eyes. He looked completely used up.

Dan did not bother to undress before plunging into the soft king-sized bed in his hotel room. He felt ashamed to have wanted to sleep so badly, but it felt so good to just lie there with his eyes closed and to think of nothing. His conscious told him he should be thinking of his girls, not worrying with what pleased him. They were in the ground, cold and alone and here he was relaxing in a very fine hotel. His mistakes cost them both their lives yet there he was cozy and fine. It made him sick. He did not want comfort. He wanted the agony he rightly deserved. Still so, he slept, and he did not wake until early Saturday afternoon.

Days turned to weeks, then months, and all the while his conscience chastising him for anything perceived as pleasure, or fun. He rarely ate, regularly drank, and often slept for more than 12hrs at a time. Dan remained at the hotel, but he knew that even the good graces of Mr. Langford were finite. There was no purpose for Dan, and it was killing him slowly. He had nothing to live for and it showed. His room was disgusting and stank of alcohol and body odor. His clothes, sometimes worn for a week or more without washing.

Dan had been on short-term disability since April, but it was mid-October, and his benefit was coming to an end. He would need to return to work or forfeit his employment. There was no decision to be made. Dan already knew that he would never return to work, and he would never return to his former home. He had put it up for sale during the summer and closed on the sale earlier in the month. Mr. Langford, again very generously, offered to pay movers to box and transport his belongings so that Dan would not have that burden. Dan had it all put in rental storage. He needed none of it and would have simply left it with the house had the buyers been willing. The only item Dan took from the house since the day Shelly died was the .357 revolver, she used to kill herself. That item, he still had need of.

In December, Dan spoke with Mr. Langford for the last time. Dan had made the decision to go home, to his childhood home, the following spring, and told Mr. Langford that he would pay for his own hotel until then. He'd already done more than enough for Dan. Of course, Mr. Langford would have none of it, and paid the full amount that day to cover through the end of April.

Dan thanked him again for his generosity and kindness and wished him well.

"Dan, if there's anything that I can ever do for you, you know where to find me. Best of luck to you."

It was near Christmas, and for Dan, an especially hard time. Seeing all the lights, and decorations, and Christmas trees, and restaurants filled with happy families made Dan feel so alone. Christmas was once his favorite time of the year, but was no more, as anything reminding him of his girls was simply torturous.

Becky loved Christmas. She was one of the few children that loved it, not for the gifts, but for the giving, and Shelly was the exact same. The greatest joy for them was when they could tell from someone's eyes that the gift was truly perfect. Two years ago, they could not contain themselves they were so excited for Dan to open his gift. He had made mention of a particular watch he liked while they were strolling through the mall but decided not to buy it because of the price. It was a fine watch. Handsome and large enough to not look out of place on Dan's oversized wrist. The girls devised a scheme to distract Dan, so that Shelly could run back to the store and buy it for him. Just a little cuteness from Becky and a white lie from Shelly was enough to leave Dan suspecting nothing. She dragged Dan into the pet store and began explaining to him why each of the toys she picked up was not a good one for Max.

"This one's too hard. It will hurt Max's teeth."

"What about this one."

"Nooooo. Daddy! That's for tiny dogs. Max is too big for that one. Don't be silly."

When Dan opened his gift on Christmas day, he was genuinely surprised and delighted to see the watch. The look on his face was the best part of Christmas that year for Shelly and Becky. They had the perfect gift for Dad, and they were so very proud.

After the call to Mr. Langford, Dan showered for the first time in two days and shaved for the first time in seven. It was late in the afternoon, and another hotel dinner was not very appetizing, so he walked downtown in search of a place to eat. Several blocks down the way, he arrived at a local bar and grill he had been to a few times before.

For dinner, he mostly drank at the bar. For several hours he sat and drank, occasionally losing himself in the game on the TV in the corner. He had never cared much about Basketball, but it was impressive to see how athletic humans could be. Some of the players seemed in danger of striking their heads on the hoop, they jumped so high. That was not something in Dan's skillset. He was tall but built like a Clydesdale not a Thoroughbred. Built to work not play.

His evening changed abruptly the moment the unfortunate gentleman took a seat next to him. Dan had in his hand the four tiny black and white photos of himself with Becky. He wasn't sure why he tortured himself by staring at the pictures, but they seemed to find their way into his hands every time he drank.

"She sure is a cute little thing, ain't she? I bet she has all the boys chasing her!" he said as he slapped Dan on the shoulder and sat down beside him.

Such a regrettable way for him to phrase it. The poor guy nearly verbatim quoted Mason Langford's comments at the mall the day he took Becky.

"You sure are a cute little thing, aren't you?" he said, as he leaned down and gently grabbed Becky's chin. "I bet you have all the boys chasing you!" Dan could see him with perfect clarity grabbing Becky by the chin and smiling that hideous smile, and in an instant Dan was to his feet.

He may not have been much at basketball, but by the way the man's head bounced off the bar, a person might have thought otherwise. The impact broke the man's nose and blood splattered the front of Dan's shirt. The man was practically unconscious from the blow, but Dan did not relent. He grabbed the man by the front of his shirt and drew back his massive fist, striking him squarely in his already grotesquely disfigured nose. The man was out cold, and Dan pushed him from the barstool and onto the floor.

The entire room was speechless with all eyes locked on Dan. No one moved and no one said a word as he laid a twenty-dollar bill on the bar and stumbled for the door. The insentient man lay motionless on the floor as Dan stepped over him. He looked down at the crumpled-up body and wondered apathetically whether he had killed him or not.

He did not make it a full block from the bar when the police caught up to him. The second he exited the building, a half a dozen people called 9-1-1. The two officers first to arrive approached, guns drawn. The 9-1-1 calls reported an enormous man killing someone with his bare hands, moments earlier and they were not taking any chances.

"Get on the ground, NOW!"

Dan complied. By then he had cooled off some, and he knew he had made a grave mistake. Even so, the damage was already done. He was on his way to jail, and probably for a long time. He spent the night there, and most of the next day before someone, probably Mr. Langford, made his bale. Thankfully, the man Dan assaulted did not die, though his face was seriously mangled. Along with a broken nose, the man's maxillary bone was broken in multiple places. He was admitted to the hospital the night before and would require several surgeries to repair his face.

Thanks to one final act of kindness from Mr. Langford, Dan spent only 90 days in jail for his crime. The actual cost of his indiscretion came from the expenses he had to pay for the reconstruction of his victim's face. Dan cashed out his entire 401K and his savings account, which included the $80,000 he had just made on the sale of his house. When the bill was paid, Dan was left with $7,000 to his name.

Dan was released from the county jail on April 7th, and so returned to the hotel to collect his few belongings. He was leaving the city forever. He was going home.

Chapter 5
Going Home

Driving down that old gravel road brought back pleasant memories for Dan. Some from his childhood, and others of his long stays in the summertime with his family. Before his father passed away, two years prior, the three of them would visit Randall for a week every year, either in May or early June. It was a very long drive, but one that the trio enjoyed. Dan and Shelly would play a variety of travel games and comment occasionally on beautiful scenery, as if seeing it for the first time. Becky sat in the back imagining the fun to be had in the coming days. As the gravel dust from the road bellowed up behind the vehicle, Becky would stare out the back window and imagine the dust to be exhaust from the rocket they were riding to a far-away world. One where it was just the three of them, and Pappy, and fun.

She loved Pappy's place. It was a place like no other to her, where she and Max could run wild, and scream, and bark, and play, and forget about everything else in the world. For Dan and Shelly, it was a week of rest. A time for them to unwind and enjoy the slowness of country life. Dan had always imagined himself and Shelly one day retiring out there, sitting on the front porch in the evenings, with a sweet tea in hand, simply enjoying the peace and quietness that could only be experienced in a place such as that.

The drive to his parent's old farm was indeed a long one. Dan had turned off the highway some ways back and had not seen another house in more than 15 miles. Out there, the land was still divided into "sections", perfect squares of 640 acres divided by intersecting gravel roads. From above, the land looked like a giant checkerboard of green, spoiled only by the occasional windings of a creek or small river weaving their way through the landscape.

Dan's ancestors homesteaded out there. He was the sole heir to the square mile of land left to him by his father. To most the folks in the city, 640 acres was enormous, and seemed like far more land than any one family could maintain or would want to for that matter. For the people that Dan had worked with, 1 acre was a very large property, and more than enough for a residence. Not so for the ranchers in Dan's old township. His 640-acre tract was tiny compared to most. Men in that part of the country owned tens of thousands of acres. Entire survey townships, or 36 square miles, perhaps more, owned by a single family, with not a neighbor in sight. Massive amounts of land with nothing but green grass, sparsely scattered forests, and cattle. Lots and lots of cattle.

The wind blew hard out there, making the fields of grass dance about, sometimes causing the blades of grass to bow synchronously to Dan as he passed. So green too, and the blue sky above the fields contrasted so sharply and beautifully. It was a perfect day, and Dan was feeling better just from experiencing it. He wasn't happy, he imagined he would never be again, but the sights and sounds of his ancestral home did help to ease his pain.

It had been almost a year since Dan buried his girls, but the pain and guilt still festered inside him. He had hoped that him and Max could build some semblance of a life out there. An existence that did not consist solely of misery, and seeing the green grasses of home created a tiny, yet real, sense of hope inside Dan. He did not deserve to be happy, and he knew this, but he wanted the remainder of his life to have some sort of purpose. Perhaps, he would find that purpose down that dusty road.

The homestead had not changed much since his childhood. The same rusty gate, long out of service, greeted him from the edge of the drive. Barely visible, it had been pushed open long ago, and left along the side of the driveway for the weeds to consume. Dan could remember closing that gate a thousand times as a kid. Randall insisted it remain closed, and locked, at all times, and Dan served as the automatic gate opener. He would hand Dan the key as they pulled up and say, "Hop out and get that for me, Danny. Lock it back once I'm through." Every time he would say those exact words, as if he feared Dan would forget the process altogether if not given regular instruction. Dan was never quite sure if the gate was for the containment of the cattle, or the prevention of uninvited guests. Randall was a solitary fellow and valued his privacy more than most, so the latter reason was the most probable.

From the road Dan could make out the roof of his parent's home, though it was quite a distance away. As he turned in the drive, the forgotten rumble of tires passing over the slats of a cattle guard, jiggled his belly as well as Max's slouching jaws. Dan chuckled at this for a moment and tapped Max on the head.

"We're home boy. No more tiny lawns and leashes for you. You can run for miles out here. Remember?" He smiled, for perhaps the first time in a year, as he petted Max's head. Max did remember, and as he raised himself in the seat to look about, the excited whimpers and fidgeting told Dan so.

Max's 90-day stay at a large kennel outside the city was harder on him than Dan's jail time. Max had lost considerable weight during the time and appeared to be suffering from what could best be described as depression. He was lying in the back of the kennel, curled up in a ball with his head down, when Dan arrived. Exactly as he had been for the previous 90 days. At hearing Dan's voice, Max jumped to his feet and bolted across the enclosure. The attendant seemed startled and confused by the energy that seemed to have come from nowhere. The pitifully silent and timid dog he had known for 3-months had been replaced in an instant by a ball of life. He was so excited he nearly cleared the six-foot fence and was wagging his nub-of-a-tail so violently his entire rear end was swaying. Seeing Max again made Dan happy too, though he was less animated by the reunion.

In front of the little farmhouse was a large horseshoe shaped pond Randall had dug when Dan was a kid. Probably 4 or 5-acres total, and deep on the south side. Like the rest of the place, it was in need of serious maintenance. The algae had taken over, covering the entire pond in a thick green slime. Around the edges, weeds as tall as Dan's shoulders blocked any access to the pond.

The wooden dock appeared rotten and rickety. A quick survey of the pond, and Dan knew he had his work cut out for him.

The pond was quite nasty as far as Dan was concerned, but after the long drive it was extremely inviting to Max. As soon as Dan stopped the truck, Max leapt over his lap and out the door, headed straight for the dock. He plunged into the lake, and Dan could do nothing but roll his eyes and sigh at the thought of how nasty and smelly Max would be. For this reason, Max would spend his first night on the farm outdoors, whining and scratching at the door until dawn.

The long drive had exhausted Dan, and when he had unloaded the essentials from his truck, he flopped down on the dusty couch in the living room and slept. He did not wake until sometime the following morning and would have slept longer had it not been for the unrelenting whines from Max. His dog had been alone for too long, and although Dan was no more than 15 feet from the dog all night, Max could not see him and therefore lamented. Dan opened the front door for Max and sleepily turned back around towards the couch. He would have laid back down, but Max beat him to the old couch and was already occupying half of it. He accepted this, and took his place beside Max, where he dozed off again for another hour or so.

Dan felt refreshed when he awoke the second time. He had energy to spare and felt like getting something accomplished.

"Max, let's take a look around this old place, and see what we got." Max cocked his head to one side and looked at Dan, as if trying unsuccessfully to understand the command. "Let's go boy." Dan slapped his leg, as he stood up from the couch, which was an all too familiar command for Max. He sprung from the couch eagerly and followed Dan into the kitchen.

After a quick breakfast and a tour of the house, Dan considered hiring a cleaning service to get the house in livable condition. It had been empty for two years and between the bugs and the dust, Dan wasn't sure if he wanted to tackle that task.

Shelly would have had that place looking new in a day or so. She could have done it and still worked a full shift at the hospital. Dan stared at the mess and marveled at how much Shelly had actually done for him. She worked full-time, kept a near immaculate house, did the laundry, cooked supper almost every night, and tended to all of Becky's needs. Doctor's and Dentist's appointments, piano practice, and bedtime stories. She did it all, always without complaint, and never really noticed by Dan until that very moment.

Almost inaudible he mumbled aloud, "I'm sorry Shelly. I should have appreciated you more. You did so much for us, and I didn't even realize...I'm so sorry, honey."

Dan had to shove the back door open with his shoulder. The old six-pane door was wedged to the door frame due to the sagging floor, but he nudged it a little too hard, and one of the panes fell from the door and onto the covered back porch scattering glass to the edges. The old porch was weathered, but very agreeable to Dan. It covered the entire length of the back of the house and had 4 old wooden rocking chairs spaced across it. A wonderful place it would make for Dan and Max to relax. Most of the paint was gone from the wood of the deck, and some boards were so rotten Dan could have put his foot through them with little effort, but he liked it all the same. The old home needed a lot of work, but that was fine with Dan. All he needed was time, and fortunately that was something Dan had plenty of.

He stepped off the porch and noticed it for the first time since his return. There, across the backyard, was the old dogwood tree that Becky loved so much. It was pretty, and blooming, and the pedals were falling to the ground covering it like a thin dusting of snow. It was growing near the entrance to a small pasture Randall had used to separate bottle-fed calves. The lot was a perfect square as far as Dan could tell, and not more than four or five acres. It was lined on the sides and back by heavily overgrown fencerows. Small trees and brush had turned the once tidy woven wire fences into a 10ft wide wall of tangled limbs and vines. The front of the lot was overgrown as well, though not nearly as much as the other three sides. Inside the pasture was a mix of tall weeds and brush, so thick that Dan would need a dozer to clear it properly.

Dan stared intently at the old dogwood as he made his way across the yard. He sat down under the blooming branches and leaned his back against its trunk. Becky used to sit there, just as Dan was and play with Max as he bounced about. Dan leaned his head back and closed his eyes as he pictured Becky playing under the tree. Year after year, her and Max growing a little at a time. It was a good memory, and one that made Dan smile as he sat in the shade of the tree.

A few moments with his head leaned against the tree, and Dan was asleep once again, but not for long this time. Max wouldn't allow it.

"Ah, Max!! Really? Come on!!" Dan jumped to his feet, banging his head on a low hanging branch on his way up, spitting repeatedly as he scolded his dog. At the first sound of Dan snoring, Max had sprinted back to the dogwood tree and proceeded to lick every square inch of Dan's face. It only took a second for him to wake, but a second was long enough for Max to completely soak his face.

Dan wiped his face with the tail of his shirt and continued with his tour around the property. It was interesting to him how the grown-up fencerows around that little pasture seemed to separate it completely from the rest of the world. Had it not been for the 16ft gated entrance by the dogwood, he would not have been able to see the field at all.

"Maybe I'll clean it up and put a couple calves out there." Dan mumbled to himself.

He made his way around the left side of the small pasture to an enormous and tall equipment barn where Randall kept all his machinery. The barn was in considerably better shape than the house, and it was easy to tell that it was most important to Randall. All his tools and equipment meticulously cleaned and stored with great care. Everything was in its designated spot, floors were swept clean, and Randall had even decorated the walls with old filling station signs he had collected throughout the years. The barn was where Randall lived. He only slept in the house. Well, at least sometimes. Apparently, he slept in the barn as well. Randall had finished out a small corner in the front of the barn, making it into a makeshift apartment, complete with a full bathroom, and kitchenette. It too was pristine compared to the old house, and it would be Dan and Max's residence while they made their renovations.

Dan worked throughout the spring and into the summer on the homestead. Diligently laboring to bring the property back to its former splendor. To support himself, he took a part time job at the feed store in the neighboring town. Between that, and the money he made from leasing some of his land, he had just enough to get by.

He started with the house, which took him 2 months to get in order. Shelly would have marveled at his inefficiency, though he was proud just to have finished it at all. By the time the house was livable, Dan and Max had become attached to the barn and continued to live there. Dan stayed busy through the summer working on the farm. If he wasn't there, he was at the feed store, always working, never stopping. He worked from before sunrise to after sunset every day, and it never bothered him. To stop, gave him time to think, and time to think meant thinking about his girls. Something that simply hurt too much, so he kept busy to keep from despairing.

Winter came though and brought with it time. Idle time for Dan. The days grew short, the nights long, and the work withered. He tried to stay busy at the feed store, but there was only so much work available. 20hrs a week left a lot of time for Dan to think, and idle hands are the devil's playground.

As the dreary winter months dragged on, Dan's disposition grew despondent. Dan had picked up the habit of reading the Bible while he sat in county jail the year prior, and continued to read, but faith was something of which Dan had little.

He would recite the verse from the book of Psalms daily, hoping that it would lead to fulfillment and purpose.

Psalms 27 :13-14

"[13] I had fainted unless I had believed to see the goodness of the Lord in the land of the living.

[14] Wait on the Lord: be of good courage, and he shall strengthen thine heart: wait, I say, on the Lord."

Dan was waiting, but his patience was dissolving rapidly. By early spring, Dan was in full blown depression. Thoughts of suicide were behind every thought in his head, and he was inching ever more closely to taking that step. Ending the pain sounded refreshing to him. To be nothing and feel nothing would be a repose.

Birthdays, Holidays, and his wedding anniversary were difficult days for Dan, but no day brought about such misery as April 14th. It was the day, two years previous, when Mason Langford stole everything from Dan. The day his life withered and died, and the day that would never let Dan go. Dan knew what day it was the instant Max woke him, and the moment he woke was the moment he wept. He laid in the bed most of the morning sobbing and remembering, Max loyally lying at his side the entire time. Most days he tried not to remember, but on the 14th of April, Dan felt he needed to remember. To remember what he had done and to remember the pain.

It was no use. His life had no meaning, nor would it ever. Dan was finished, and what better day to see it done than the day of his daughter's disappearance. He had spent the last two years of his life in total anguish, hoping for something better, but knowing he deserved worse. Trying to move on, yet still stuck in the very same spot. Perhaps if he killed himself, God would forgive him. Perhaps He would allow Dan into His Kingdom, as unworthy as Dan knew he was. Perhaps he could see his girls again.

"That's why Jesus died, right? He died so my sins could be forgiven. If that is true, I'm better off dead anyway. Forgive me Father and let me come home. Please Jesus...please..."

Dan's mind was made. He would die that day, though he could not sentence his best friend to the same fate. Max had done nothing wrong, and he had plenty of life left in him. The girl at the feed store really liked Max, and Max seemed to like her. Dan could ask her to watch him for a few days. Surely, she would take care of him once he was gone. She had to.

It was hard to tell Max goodbye for the last time. Kelly, the cashier at the feed store, thought it weird that Dan leaving Max with her for a couple of days would bring him to tears, but what business was it of hers. She knew Dan was different, a quiet man with a soft heart, and awkward around most folks, but she also knew him to be a good man, so she was happy to help him.

Dan parted ways with Max and headed back to what would be his exit from the world. He was happy. Genuinely happy for the first time in two years. If the Gospels were true, he would be in Paradise that very day, and he could hardly wait.

"Take me home, Father." He kept repeating as he sped down the gravel roads towards his farm. Taking care of Max was his only preparation and that was done. Nothing else mattered. What did he care of what happened to the farm? It had been nothing but work and toil for him anyway and Paradise awaited him. A paradise where he would see his girls again. He could hardly wait.

When he stepped out of the truck, he stretched his arms out widely and closed his eyes as he turned his head to the sky. The big stretch, and sun hitting his face made him feel amazing. A nice breeze blowing across the lawn and onto his face made the moment that much more marvelous. He stayed there for several seconds before relaxing and letting out a satisfied sigh.

Dan was in no mood for wasting time. He had waisted two years and that was long enough. He should have done this the day Shelly died, and he had thought about it in the moment. Maybe he was too much of a coward then. He held the revolver in his hand that day, but he could not pull the trigger. It would be different this time.

The old dogwood tree was in full bloom again. It was beautiful, and there was no other place on earth Dan would have rather been than sitting in its shade. He crawled up under the tangle of branches and blooms and sat staring towards the little pasture he had worked so hard to restore. He had done well with it, and Dan hoped that there would be a pasture like that one waiting for him on the other side.

"Father, forgive me…accept me into Your Kingdom."

Dan whispered those words before taking one last gulp up air. No more wasting time, he was going home. Dan raised the revolver and pressed it to the side of his head, and without hesitation pulled the trigger.

Chapter 6
A New Plan

With his eyes still shut tightly, Dan wondered if he was dead. He knew he had pulled the trigger, but he had not felt or heard anything. He pulled the trigger again. Still nothing. He opened his eyes and looked at the silver revolver in his hand with agitation.

"What in the hell…" he mumbled as he released the cylinder to find six empty holes in place of his .357 Magnum cartridges. Dan sighed in disgust as he tossed the gun out into the grass in front of him and began crying again. A moment ago, he was on his way to Paradise, now, he would have to wait. He had no ammunition for the gun, and the closest store was 30 miles away. Several minutes passed as he contemplated hanging himself, but as he thought, a tiredness fell upon him that he could not overcome. The tidal wave of emotions he had just experienced had drained him of his energy.

Hanging would certainly get the job done, but ultimately Dan knew he did not possess the courage. It would have to be a bullet, quick and painless, and it would have to wait until he awoke again.

There was something about sitting against that tree that made Dan fade to sleep. It seemed that every time he settled against its base, something he had done regularly over the past year, he would nap, sometimes for hours. It was a deep sleep on that occasion though, and Dan dreamt vividly. He saw his girls in Heaven, both happy and safe. Their faces were bright, almost too bright to make out their appearance, but Dan could feel them more than he could see them. They were walking on clouds of light as they spoke with a Man he could not recognize. Dan did not know him, but he could feel His love for the girls in his own body, and that love gave Dan an indescribable comfort that he had never felt before.

He wanted to join them, but there was a great void between them and himself with no way to bridge it. Dan stood at the edge and watched as Shelly and Becky and the unnamed Man moved about, following a bright path that led further and further away, until they were beyond his sight.

The dream turned dark as the three exited his view. Mason Langford appeared before him, or rather, a devilish form of Mason appeared, and for a moment, Dan could see through Mason's eyes. Mason was inside his apartment, the night he took Becky, and he was doing unspeakable things to Becky. Dan saw first-hand the torment she went through. Listened as she begged for Daddy to save her, and he felt the pain as if it were his own as Mason mercilessly beat and raped her. It was a moment devoid of all humanity, and as Dan watched his blood began to boil. He tried desperately to stop Mason, but he was trapped inside his body. He could only watch through Mason's eyes as he ravaged his precious daughter.

A moment later, and the two were back at the edge of the void. Mason stood facing the expanse, as Dan was rushing behind him trying with futility to grasp him. As he approached Mason, Dan's body slowed, then froze, leaving him unable to move or speak. Mason's attention was focused on the path taken by Becky and Shelly. He did not move or speak for some time, seeming to either be unaware of Dan's presence or simply disinterested. Dan stood frozen and helpless, and as he peered at Mason, a wrath like a raging fire burned inside him. One that he knew could never be extinguished. Dan not only wanted Mason's life, but he also wanted his soul. He wanted to destroy all of him.

Mason's eyes were jet black when he turned to face Dan. The smile on his face was the same one he wore two years ago at the mall, but somehow different. It was a smile that in life unsettled Dan, but now it altogether terrified him. His teeth were sharpened to a point and blood ran from the corners of his eyes as he pointed his finger at Dan. A finger that was not human. Twice as long as it should have been in fact, with a long and curved, dirty claw at the tip. A forked tongue emerged from his mouth and slithered about as Mason began to speak.

"It is too late, Dan. We took them as you stood by and did nothing. We took them as we will take all the others, and we will have them for eternity. You cannot stop us Dan, for we are many." Mason turned towards the void and leapt forward, rushing, with immense speed towards Becky and Shelly's path. Dan could only watch as Mason turned to face him one last time with his terrible and demonic smile. Down the path and out of sight he went, leaving Dan alone, with nothing but the storm inside him raging.

Dan awoke, sweaty and shaking. The dream was still with him, and the wrath he felt in his dream had followed him back to reality. Dan no longer wanted to die, he wanted to kill. He wanted to kill them all, whoever or whatever they were.

"We are many? ...Then many will die!" As Dan spoke those words, he began to see what his purpose was to be. There would be no justice for Becky or Shelly in him killing himself, and justice was what Dan wanted above all. For evil to reap its due reward, and Dan could make that happen. The evil that possessed Mason Langford killed his girls. It not only possessed Mason, but many others who shared in that same evilness. Many that were free and unpunished, and many that deserved the same punishment as Mason. It was too late for Dan to exact his justice on Mason perhaps, but there was still time to punish the others, and he would do just that. The burning desire to do so was consuming Dan that very moment.

He would rid the world of some of its evil. He would do it for Becky and Shelly, and in the place of the ugliness of those evil men, he would create something beautiful. Something for Becky. As Dan sat under the dogwood, he remembered back to the day in the morgue. He remembered the terrible images of Becky's lifeless body, her grey and hollow eyes, and he remembered the things he had said. Dan had said in his rage fueled tirade that if it were possible, he would have killed Mason Langford 100 times over. So, 100 it would be. Dan would take

100 lives of men deserving of such a violent death. 100 of the most vile and evil men would perish for what they had done to his daughter.

Days passed as Dan contemplated his future. Would he actually do it? Could he do it? 100 "murders" before being caught sounded quite impossible the more he thought about it. He did not think of it as murder though. He had convinced himself that what he was planning was just, and good, and a due reward for those who had somehow skirted the justice system. For the ones who were allowed to go free after destroying another's life, he would balance the scales.

On the following Monday, Dan and his newly reunited best friend, Max, were standing by the old dogwood tree once again. Dan was peering out across the small square pasture he had so meticulously restored while Max sat staring contently at Dan. It was a pretty, little field, and Dan wanted to use it to memorialize his daughter, though a field, pretty as it was, would be an unworthy tribute. He was deep in thought when the little white bloom fell from the old tree and landed perfectly on Dan's right shoulder. It was perfect, and what better way to remember Becky than with the tree that she loved so much. Dan would turn the small field into an orchard full of dogwoods. 100 dogwoods to be exact. In 10 rows of 10 perfectly spaced trees, arranged such that in the springtime, the pasture would look as though it were covered with fresh snow. A beautiful picture it would be, and one that Becky would have loved to see.

It would not really be an orchard though; it would be a more like a garden...Rebecca's Garden. And so, Dan set out to turn his old pasture into something beautiful, for his Becky.

"How would I ever expect to kill 100 people before getting caught?" Dan thought to himself as he walked across the green pasture. "It's ridiculous. No one can do that, Dan, and you know it. You would have to be perfect, and you're far from that. After two or three, the Feds would get involved and they would be hunting a serial killer. That's what those guys live for, catching serial killers. That's how they make a name for themselves. The feds loved nothing so much as a hunt for a serial killer. No, you could never do it...unless..."

A tingling sensation danced inside Dan's belly as he realized it could be done...that it would be done. Dan stared out across the empty field as the plan began to take shape in his mind. First, He would have to ensure he could never be traced back to the scene of a crime. Daniel Stoker could never be there. He would always be hundreds of miles away. To do this, he would need fake identities, and he knew exactly how to get them.

Secondly, and most importantly, there could be no trace of a crime at all. This was crucial, the most important part, and he would need exceptional planning to make it happen. Planning was everything, and planning was something that Dan had plenty of experience with. He had always been detail-oriented, meticulous, almost to a fault. Every action he took would be planned with the utmost care.

The victims would simply vanish. Dan knew most would be on parole, or probation, or bond, or some sort of watchlist. He would make the authorities believe his victims had jumped bail, left town, or disappeared to get away from the authorities. The idea, for Dan was to have the police looking for a felon in flight, rather than a serial killer. If he spaced them out over years, over the entire country, without redundancies or similarities, they would never suspect any murders.

Hundreds if not thousands of criminals disappear every year. The cops never find some of them, and that is exactly what his victims would do, which meant there could be no struggle, there could be no blood, and there could be no body left for the police. Dan already knew where the bodies would go. As he said before, he would remove some of the ugliness from the world and replace it with something beautiful.

He would plant their corpses in Rebecca's Garden. No one would ever know. He had no neighbors, he never had visitors, and the entire garden would be virtually invisible unless a person were to actually be in it. The ugliness of those perverse men would then be part of something truly beautiful, and Dan thought that to be the way it ought to be.

Dan worked out many of the details over the following two months as he constructed the garden of trees. The old lady at the local nursery thought he had lost his mind when he told her he wanted 100 dogwood saplings, but she ordered them all the same. He laid out a grid inside the pasture, taking care so that it would be perfect, with every tree precisely where it should be. Each row was to be spaced allowing for flower lined walkways between them. Space enough for each of his victims to be buried next to their tree.

By mid-July, Dan had transformed the old pasture into an unquestionably splendid garden, full of color, and beauty, and life. Above the entrance, Dan had purchased and installed a large arched sign made of wrought iron. From the twisted iron bars inside the arch read the words "Rebecca's Garden". For Dan, it was the perfect finishing touch. The garden was for her and belonged to her, and thus should bear her name.

With the culmination of the garden, Dan switched his focus towards outlining his plan. His first step was to create multiple false identities. It may seem like a difficult task to do, but for Dan it was far too easy. Laughable, really. Half the states in the country were providing ID's and Driver's Licenses to undocumented immigrants with virtually no way of verifying a person's identity.

He started in New York. It was well over a 24hr drive for him, but from recent national news, he was sure he would have no trouble there. And he was right. In one day, he had obtained two driver's licenses from the two county courthouses he visited. Few questions were asked, and when they were, he feigned ignorance and illiteracy. His fluency in Spanish was invaluable during this process. His persona would always be the same. He posed as an immigrant from, where else but, Monterrey, Mexico. Just a hardworking, migrant worker looking to live a better life like so many others.

Dan's mother was Italian, and he favored his mother, more so than his father, in appearance. He had inherited her straight black hair, and dark complexion, though he was unsure where his size came from. Both parents were small in stature, unlike Dan, who appeared to be a giant to most folks. He was large, no doubt, but he easily passed as a Latino, at least he did to the people who mattered at the time. Nonetheless, his appearance and fluency gained him twelve false identities from ten different states in less than two weeks. He was ready to move forward with his plan.

One of Dan's identities purchased a 100,000V taser from a store in Georgia that summer. He was sure it was enough to incapacitate a man, but still he tried it on himself. He was correct, and ill-advised for being his own guinea pig. His head hurt terribly for the rest of the day, and he had a mark on his arm for the following two weeks.

His plan was simple. Take his victim down with the taser, restrain him and kill him. But, before his victim should die, they would assist in the cover-up. Sending texts to friends or family, signaling they were leaving. Writing notes for their parole officers, taunting them. Sometimes emptying bank accounts, and Dan would even pack bags for them to sell the story. Anything that could make it look like a fleeing felon, he would do. He just had to get the body back to his farm without detection, and he would be in the clear.

All that was left was to pick his first victim. Little did he know when he started the endeavor that the hardest part would be to whittle the candidates down to just one. There were so many. So many, he could not believe it. How could all those men be free? The more he discovered, the firmer his commitment to fulfilling his agenda became. He sifted through mountains of information, detailing the crimes of each man, and thinking as he went that he would have no issue sending any one of them, or all of them, to hell. He thought it would be his pleasure as well as his purpose. These men were truly the scum of the earth, and Dan was dumbfounded that any of them were free to walk the streets. Probation for sexually assaulting an 8year old? Really? For harming a child in the most horrific way, leaving them scarred forever, a man should get probation?

"In a just world, this would not happen. In a just world, a man would die for such a thing." Dan thought, as he read through the list, offense after offense after offense. He recalled as he read, a passage from the Bible:

"It were better for him that a millstone were hanged about his neck, and he cast into the sea, than that he should offend one of these little ones." Luke 17:2

And it would have been better for the 100 chosen by Dan, had they merely drowned. Their deaths would come much slower, and much more painfully by his hands. He would make sure of it. He swore it.

As Dan continued researching, it occurred to him that perhaps these States wanted him to do what he was doing. All the information he needed was at the tips of his fingers as he perused each State's sex offender registry. It was as if they were his accomplices in his mission. They gave him everything he needed, names, convictions, and most importantly, current addresses of each offender. All he had to do was pick one and go to work.

The problem was the sheer number of candidates, literally thousands and thousands of perverts, and all over the country. He was surprised, and somewhat startled, at how many there were within 100 miles of his farm. There were more than two dozen registered offenders in his rural, and sparsely populated county alone. Some, of course, were minor offenders, but there were a couple on the list that tempted Dan. In the end, he decided that the farther from home, the better, and continued his search.

It took him days to decide, but Dan finally settled on a particularly despicable individual by the name of David Eadon. David had spent the last 15years in prison for snatching a young boy from his bed and raping him so violently he nearly killed the boy. And David had intended to kill him. He thought the boy was dead when he left his battered body lying in the mud. Had the boy not survived, David may have never been caught. The child was found unconscious the next day in a drainage ditch a few miles from Portland and was rushed to the local hospital.

The boy's testimony helped send David to prison, but the damage had already been done. One year, to the day, after the assault, the parents of the young child found him hanged from his bedpost with his own shoestrings. He had spent the last year suffering from fear and depression so intense, he had chosen death instead of a life of mental torment and misery. David killed that boy. Just as much as Mason Langford had killed Becky, he had taken that boy's life, and Dan would balance the scales. Why did David deserve to go on living…and for more than 15years!…after what he had done to that little boy. No, he deserved death, and it was soon to be delivered.

Dan remembered the story. He was young then, but he remembered seeing David on television. He had a smile similar to Mason's, which may have been the determining factor in Dan's decision to select him. The story made national news for months, and when he saw David's picture on that website, it reminded him of the callousness he displayed during his trial. The only regret David had was getting caught and it showed. Recalling the trial only added to Dan's anger, and it solidified his decision that David would be #1.

Chapter 7

#1

Dan was nearly as disgusted by the filth inside David's home as he was by his criminal offenses. He had never witnessed anything like it, and he wondered how any human could be so repulsive. The stench was so powerful, Dan could hardly bear to breath. The scent so thick and obnoxious he could taste it. Garbage and rotten food littered the floors of every room, providing plenty of food for the thousands of bugs that crawled about. Empty Whiskey bottles and beer cans decorated the tops of every surface in the dwelling. There was nothing on the walls other than the faded and flaking dull grey paint. The only furniture in the house was a leather recliner that looked to be 30 years old, a small metal TV stand, a kitchen table with two chairs, and a urine-soaked twin sized mattress in one of the bedrooms.

"I should just shoot this nasty son-of-a-bitch as soon as he gets here and leave him lay." Dan thought as he toured through the house.

David lived just outside of a small town in Northeast Oregon. He had moved there when he was paroled to "rediscover himself". He worked part-time at the local grocery store, bagging goods for customers, and spent the rest of his time drinking whiskey at his residence. Dan had been there for about a week, and David's routine changed little from day-to-day. He either went to work, then back home, stopping only for liquor, or he slept the entire day when not working. He had no transportation, and he had no friends. It was a pathetic existence, and for a moment Dan thought the greater punishment might have been to allow him to continue living that way.

It was two o'clock in the afternoon when Dan entered the residence through the unlocked back door. David usually arrived back home by 3pm, so Dan waited in the living room impatiently. The smell was overpowering and by 2:30pm he thought he would have to wait outside or risk vomiting all over his first crime scene. He was headed to the back door when he heard David talking to himself as he walked up the drive. The man seemed to be in a pleasant mood for the moment, probably due to the half empty fifth of whiskey he was toting.

David stumbled through his front door and fell into a pile of overly ripe garbage in the hallway, before realizing he was not alone. He slurred a few indiscernible words at Dan before he was put to sleep by the taser. Apparently, David was more than a little drunk at 2:30 in the afternoon, because he did not regain consciousness until nearly 9pm.

This gave Dan time to think. Plenty of time to think, so much so that he had almost talked himself out of his plan by the time David woke. But he woke, and at the sound of his voice,

Dan's resolve returned to him. David's mouth was just as filthy as his home, and full of hate and arrogance. He sat, cursing everything under the sun as Dan walked through the back door. Dan had secured him to one of the kitchen chairs while he was passed out and would have gagged him too but feared he might choke on his own vomit if gagged. He wanted him dead, but not that way. Dan wanted all his victims to know why they were dying and who was killing them. Choking in his sleep was no justice for David.

It had been dark outside for a while when David woke, and the crickets were making quite a racket outside the kitchen window as Dan sat down in front of David. He spit all over Dan before he could get a gag in his mouth, and that combined with the smell inside the house caused Dan to vomit on the kitchen floor. It must have amused David to see him so repulsed, since he laughed hysterically while Dan emptied the contents of his stomach.

He knew it was a mistake, but Dan's anger won out and he punched David so hard in the side of the face that one of maybe 6 or 7 teeth remaining in his head sailed across the room and skidded to a stop against a pile of trash on the kitchen floor. Blood splattered on the kitchen window, and David fell silent again. He would not come to again until midnight.

This time, David awoke already gagged. While he slept, Dan did what he could to clean up any evidence he had left but was sure he did a novice job at best.

"It doesn't matter. No one will be looking for this idiot. If I left him here it would be a month before anyone found him.

The only person that would even care at all would be the landlord when the rent went unpaid."

David opened his eyes this time to a nightmare. Dan had months to plan his actions, and he knew just what he would do to David. He remembered the way his little girl looked lying on that steel table, and before he was done with David, David would look the same. Battered body from head to toe, broken and dislocated fingers, and cold, grey, dead eyes.

Dan used a pair of cloth wrapped pliers to snap each finger on David's hands. The cloth was used to prevent David from bleeding anymore that necessary. Though he could not understand him, Dan knew that David was begging him to stop each time a bone snapped, and for just a moment he pitied him.

"If you spit on me again, I'll twist your nose from your face with this pair of pliers. Do you understand?" Dan asked looking into David's eyes for conformation as he removed the gag. David nodded and sat in silence while Dan spoke to him.

"The life of a child is worth more than 15years in prison, David. You know that, and I know that. Your punishment has been tremendously insufficient, and I have come to administer true justice to you. You do not deserve life, David, and I will be taking it from you tonight."

"I've done my time…I've paid for my crimes…"

Dan lunged forward and grasped David around the throat with both hands, squeezing so hard he nearly crushed his windpipe.

"You've paid for nothing; you piece of shit!!! Nothing!! You stole a life, and you will pay with yours!! You killed that boy, and you deserve to die, and I am here to see that it is done!!!

You are dead man, David!!" He let go of David's throat with one hand and grasped David's broken fingers with it, wringing them mercilessly. David screamed in agony and begged for mercy, but none was given. Letting go of his neck and hands, Dan began pounding David in the torso, repeatedly, until Dan could hear the bones breaking. David was again near unconsciousness, and Dan knew he would not be able to continue much longer.

"I've paid...I've paid...I've paid..." David repeated this continually as he sat slumped over in the chair.

"Almost, David. You've almost paid."

Dan retrieved the small wooden dowel and length of rope from his bag on the back porch and returned to David.

"This is for my Becky." He said as he slipped the makeshift tourniquet over David's head. David did not look up. He just kept repeating "I've paid" until the pressure around his neck prevented him to do so. Dan grabbed him by the hair on top of his head and raised him up so that he could see David's eyes.

He twisted it so tightly, David's entire face turned purple, and blood ran from his nose and eyes. David began to twitch violently as his brain was starved of oxygen. Dan continued to apply pressure on his neck until the twitching ceased, and he saw the same dead eyes he had seen in his daughter. When he was sure David had expired, he released him and let him fall to the floor. Dan sat at the kitchen table for another hour or so thinking about what he had done. His mind worked tirelessly to provide him with justification for such violence.

Although he knew David deserved the death he received, Dan could not help but feel dirty and stained with evilness, but there was no turning back. The punishment would be the same for 1 or 100, and so he would continue on. He wrapped David in heavy plastic and placed him in the trunk of his rental car. That was the riskiest part of the plan. Any unexpected problems could see him rotting in prison for the rest of his life. A minor accident, a traffic stop, a flat tire. Any one of those could be the end, and his nerves were shaken just thinking about it.

It was over 100 miles to the isolated parking lot where he left his truck. It was a good spot, and it had taken days for him to find it, but he was sure to be unnoticed as he transferred the body from the rental car to his truck's toolbox. He had modified the bottom of the box with a false floor so that even when opened, the body would remain hidden. Once David was in the truck box, his chances of getting caught diminished greatly.

After returning the car to the rental facility, Dan took three taxis to 3 different towns before having the fourth take him to his truck. While riding back to his truck, he reflected on his performance, and realized how negligent and sloppy it had been. He had done everything wrong, left evidence all over the place, and with but a little effort, a mediocre investigator would discover him. He began to sweat heavily as he thought about the consequences of his sloppiness. 1 out of 100 and he would be done for because of his carelessness. His only hope was that no one cared enough to even look for David.

Dan tipped the driver and exited the taxi about a half a mile from the lot where his truck awaited him. As he approached the truck, the terrible stench he had endured inside David's house filled his nostrils again. He could smell David's body from 10ft away, and it was not only a smell of decay, but also one of intolerable human excrement and body odor. It would be a very long drive home for Dan.

Dan drove nonstop back to his farmhouse. He had installed an auxiliary fuel tank in the bed of his truck specifically for this purpose, and he was very thankful he had thought to do so. Stopping at gas stations could have aroused suspicions, especially with the awful odor coming from the back of his truck, as well as increase the risk of someone identifying him if an investigation were launched.

The butterflies in Dan's stomach would not leave him the entire ride home. He kept going back to the moment when he lost his temper.

"That cannot happen again, Dan. Stupid, Stupid, Stupid. You left blood there for sure. What about his teeth? Did you pick all of them up? What else did you leave? So sloppy! You can't lose your temper, you just can't. We have to do this without flaw." Dan mumbled to himself as he drove down the interstate.

He knew he had made mistakes, and probably left some unintentional clues for any would-be investigator, but the thing that worried him the most, was the one bit of evidence he left there on purpose. He nearly convinced himself to drive his truck back to the house to retrieve it, but that could be even more dangerous. No, he would leave it and take the risk, but what compelled him to do so anyway? It seemed to Dan that he had left his mark, much in the same way that many other killers left their calling cards. There was no logic to it, it could only help to get him caught, but still he chose to leave it.

While waiting for David to arrive, Dan found an old Bible lying in the corner of one of the bedroom floors. It was barely visible, covered with trash and dust, but he saw the corner of it from across the room and knew immediately what it was. He pulled it from the pile of debris and dusted it off. After a few moments of contemplation, he flipped to the Gospel of Luke and circled in pen the verse of Luke: 17:2. After doing so, he returned the book to its home beneath the rubbish.

In all likelihood, it would never be discovered, Dan knew that, but still he worried. Not so much that the verse would be found, but that one of the ninety-nine others he was destined to leave would be discovered before his work could be completed. Though he knew it to be a mistake, he would leave his calling card wherever he went.

Dan arrived back at the farm just before midnight and was thoroughly exhausted, but he would not rest until David was settled. The smell emanating from his truck would only worsen the longer he stayed, and David had been in there for more than 20hrs already. Though tired, he made his way to the barn and warmed up his old Ford tractor. David would be buried in the back righthand corner of the garden.

To conserve space in Rebecca's Garden, Dan planned to bury each victim vertically behind their respective trees. To do this efficiently, he had modified an auger used to set power line poles and fitted it to the hitch and PTO of his tractor. With this adapted piece of equipment, Dan could dig a hole nearly 2 feet in diameter to a depth of about 8ft in a matter of minutes. If the hole were to be any bigger, Dan would have to do that the old-fashioned way.

Thankfully, David was a used up, frail little man, and he slid to the bottom of the hole without any resistance. It perplexed Dan that of all the hundreds, perhaps, thousands of perverts he researched online, most all of them seemed to be short and effeminate. Could their small stature have something to do with their sickness? Dan thought on this for a moment before dismissing it. No, though most appeared to be scrawny there were more than a handful he remembered to be bordering morbid obesity, and a few that were naturally large men. He looked down at the hole, and decided he should avoid those men, if possible, if for no other reason than for the sake of his back.

It was almost 2am when Dan patted the last of the dirt on David's grave, but he had one last chore before he could sleep. Inside the barn was an old engraving machine his father had purchased to help identify his equipment. There were several hundred unused tags left in the shop, each slightly larger than a dog tag used by the military. They were stainless steel tags, with a small loop of wire rope run through a hole at their corners.

So he would never forget, Dan would tag each tree, with a date, a number, a name, and on the back, the words from Luke 17:2. He knew this to be a mistake as well, but he did not care. He would be the only one to step foot in Rebecca's Garden, at least until he was gone anyway. Maybe that was it. Maybe he wanted to leave proof of what he had accomplished, but keep it hidden until his own death.

Max began pawing at the fresh dirt behind the tree as Dan hung the tag around a lower branch.

"Stop it Max, stop it. We do not dig in Rebecca's Garden." He stated bluntly as he looked down at Max with a disapproving expression. Max seemed to understand and relented.

"David Eadon. #1. I'd bet you would have preferred to be thrown into the sea. Ninety-nine to go Max...let's go to bed." Max trotted alongside Dan as they made their way back through the garden and to the barn.

Though he was as tired as he had ever been, Dan did not fall asleep as quickly as he had imagined. After a long shower, he laid on the bed with Max at his side and recounted the last couple of days, again and again. He was not worrying like before though. No, he was feeling a sense of pride...accomplishment...and purpose. He was glad David was dead, and he was glad he had been the one to kill him. Justice had finally caught up with David, and it would not be long before it caught up with #2.

Chapter 8

Taking Luis

That summer was an especially long one for Dan. He did his best to keep his mind occupied with work, either at the farm or the feed store, but the days dragged on. His inability to sleep through the night only added to long days filled with worry and anxiety. He was anxious to move on to his second target, whom he had selected only two days after burying David, but Dan knew he needed to wait, at least through the end of summer to continue. The times he was not preoccupied with envisioning the demise of #2, he was worrying as to whether or not the authorities in Oregon were closing in on him. He scoured the internet daily, looking for any article related to the disappearance of David Eadon, and each day he was relieved to find that no one seemed to care at all about his absence.

Dan enjoyed working at the local feed store. It gave him a sense of normalcy, and occasionally his mind would clear completely of all the hate and anger and sadness that possessed him as he stacked and organized the large bags of grain in the warehouse. He was also especially fond of talking with the customers as they hurriedly shuffled in and out of the store. Those farmers were always rushing, always behind schedule, but always genuinely sincere and polite. Dan imagined that those men and women were some of the friendliest he'd ever known, and he was thankful for the brief conversations with them, for without them, his only conversations occurred within his head or with Max. Yes, Dan liked it there, but he had other business to attend to, and the wait was maddening.

About 6 weeks after the murder, Dan got the green light he needed to move forward. The Oregon State Police had issued an arrest warrant for David for violating his terms of parole. That was it. They were chasing a ghost, looking for a felon on the run, exactly as Dan had believed they would. The news was very pleasing to Dan, and he immediately began plotting his next moves.

Number two would be significantly more challenging for Dan than David was, and he had almost abandoned the idea more than once, but the more he read about Luis Ortega, the stronger his conviction became. He was a vile man, without conscience, devoid of all decency, and fully in need of retribution. Luis had been arrested nearly 30 times in his life and had spent more than 10years in federal prison for assaulting and raping a teenage girl.

His convictions though were not what compelled Dan. It was the crimes he had been accused of but never tried for that motivated him. Entire families had disappeared under the direction of Luis, and rumors had circulated that he owned property in Mexico where he housed dozens of underaged girls that he trafficked around the world. The man had no conscious whatsoever, and the torture, rape, and degradation of children was nothing more than a form of entertainment to him.

Luis would be a difficult target for a couple of reasons. One, he was certain to be on the watchlist for law enforcement. It was quite possible that he was being surveilled at that very moment. The second reason, he was a known member of the Ruiz Cartel, and as far as Dan could tell, was someone of significant importance to the organization. He was sure to be surrounded by men as violent and wicked as him. Dan would quite possibly need to kill multiple individuals just to get to Luis, so planning would be critical for success.

From what Dan could gather, Luis was running drugs for the Ruiz Cartel out of El Paso, TX, so Dan prepared to visit the area and do some reconnaissance. He drove to Dallas, and using one of his alias's, rented a vehicle for the drive to San Antonio. There, he used another alias to rent the vehicle he would use to get to El Paso. Once he arrived, he used a third alias to rent a third vehicle and a hotel room for the duration of his stay.

It took him nearly two weeks, and one bar fight with a local before he ever laid eyes on Luis. In fact, Dan had all but given up on ever finding him and was heading home the following morning, when by blind luck he happened to stop by a local bar for a few drinks. It was there that he ran into Luis. It was a depressing little hole-in-the-wall dive. A place where you would expect to find the lowlifes in a town. Old and dimly lit, with a thick haze of cigarette smoke filling the entire room. The smell of alcohol, smoke, and body odor unyielding and offensive.

The establishment was out-of-the-way, and Dan was unsure of how he even came across the little bar. The parking lot was dilapidated, in need of major repairs, and was nearly pitch black, as the only light in the lot appeared to have burned out years ago. In the alley beside the bar was a single portable toilet that happened to be the most popular area in the bar. The staggering patrons of the bar formed a near continuous line outside the enclosure for most of the night, with Dan using it himself no less than 4 times.

As the night dragged on, the barroom slowly emptied until there was no one left other than Dan, the two women tending bar, and 3 or 4 drunks passed out and scattered across the room. Dan sipped his bourbon as he carried on with his usual drinking ritual. He had pulled the 4 tiny photos of Becky and himself from his front pocket a few minutes earlier and was attempting to hold back the tears as he stared, almost trance-like, at the pictures.

It was after 1am when Dan, looking through the mirror behind the bar, noticed Luis walking through the front door with two other men. By that time, Dan was intoxicated, but nowhere nearly as bad as the three men who had just arrived. They staggered to the bar and demanded shots from the bartenders in Spanish before one looked at Dan and began insulting him relentlessly in Spanish. Dan acted as though he did not understand, and after a moment, the man lost interest and resumed conversing with Luis and the other man.

Seeing Luis sobered Dan immediately and almost completely. He could not believe he had spent two weeks looking for this man, only to find him there, at that rundown little bar on the outskirts of El Paso. His mind began racing, trying to determine the best course of action. Should he hang around and follow the three when they leave? Should he just kill everyone in the room? There were no cameras at a dump like that. He was sure of it. He could do it, and most likely get away with it. No, he would not kill the innocent, he knew that. There had to be another way.

"What to do?" he thought as he stared down into his empty shot glass.

He decided to leave. Or at least, make everyone in the bar believe he had left. Dan paid his bill and stood to leave, just as the belligerent next to him grabbed him by the arm and cursed him in Spanish one last time. He again kept his head, pretended he could not understand, and headed for the door.

As Dan walked past the vehicle Luis had arrived in, he noticed the keys were left in the ignition. Apparently, murderous, drug dealing, psychopaths do not worry much of having their belongings stolen. Who would risk doing something as foolish as stealing from men like him? When he made it to his rental car, Dan sat in the seat thinking for a minute or so before driving off. He had a plan.

He drove his car a couple of blocks down the road and parked it in a used car lot on the corner. From there, he jogged back to the bar and waited outside behind the portable toilet. If the men stayed in the bar for long, Luis would eventually make his way out there, and hopefully alone. The john could not be seen from inside the bar, and Luis's car was parked just a few feet away from it. If he came out alone, Dan would take him. It was insane, but it was his plan. Perhaps he hadn't sobered as much as he had thought.

An hour passed before Luis finally filled his bladder, and when Dan saw him walk through the front door alone, butterflies began attacking his stomach. He was nervous, but also excited and ready to take a chance. He was so excited his lips and fingertips began to tingle as he waited for Luis to near.

Luis never knew what hit him. He was so ridiculously drunk he could barely walk to begin with, but the straight right Dan delivered to his chin turned the lights out completely. Luis was a small man too, and Dan had no trouble scooping him up and throwing him in the back seat of the car before driving away. The two men at the bar never even raised their heads as Dan sped out of the parking lot. They were out cold as well from the night of hard drinking.

Dan spent the rest of the night maneuvering vehicles around. He drove Luis's vehicle to his rental, where Dan tied him up and left him in the trunk of his own car. He then returned the rental vehicle to the dealership and walked the 5 miles back to the car lot where he had left Luis and the car. It was risky, but it worked out. Either the punch, or the alcohol, or the combination of the two rendered Luis lifeless until late the next morning.

By the time Luis began to stir, Dan was less than two hours from where he left his truck in Dallas. Dan could hear him cursing, then banging on the walls of the trunk, so he pulled off the interstate and stopped in a secluded area just outside of Fort Worth to deal with the situation.

With the vehicle stopped, it was clear to Dan that Luis had fully awoken and was more than agitated, by the continual banging coming from inside the trunk. Luis recoiled from the brightness of the sun as Dan popped the lid to investigate. The hangover Luis was surely suffering from was probably intensified by the sudden exposure to the light, but he quickly recovered and attempted to exit the vehicle. However, with his hands tied behind his back, that was an impossible task, and Dan simply pinned his head to the bottom with one of his hands while he informed Luis of his current situation.

"Good morning, Luis!" Dan shouted, somewhat cheerfully. "You and I have a long drive ahead of us, so I suggest you listen closely if you wish to remain conscious through it. I can set you up front with me, or you can stay back here, your choice, but if you are going to set up front, you best behave. What will it be?"

"Get me out of this trunk now, essay, and I'll kill you quickly."

"Right, I'll assume you want to ride up front with me. Just know that you mess up, and you'll be sleeping back here again before you know it. It's been a lonesome two weeks for me, and I wouldn't mind some company for the ride home, even if it's you, I guess."

Luis did not speak as Dan pulled him from the car and stood him up. He stood motionless, staring at Dan with a look that would terrify most. It was clear that Luis expected that he would kill Dan in the very near future, and Dan scoffed when he saw the hard look he was being given by Luis. Dan was nearly a foot taller than Luis and outweighed him by over 100lbs and he was certain he could crush him easily if need be.

Luis was not a large man, but he did have a very intimidating appearance about him. He stood with absolute confidence, and his small, but muscular body was covered in tattoos, most of which appeared to be Satanic to Dan. Demons and skulls and images of death covered his arms and neck, and there were multiple teardrops tattooed down both sides of his face. Yes, to most people, Luis was a very scary individual.

Dan searched his pockets and found a gigantic roll of $100 bills in them, along with a large folding knife and a bag full of some type of pills. He threw the knife and drugs into the weeds beside the car and stuffed the roll of money in his pocket as he thanked Luis.

After securing Luis in the passenger's seat with a small piece of rope, Dan returned to the trunk to close the lid, but noticed for the first time, two small black duffel bags pushed in the corner. When he opened the first bag, he could not believe his eyes. There had to have been a quarter of a million dollars in there. It was stuffed full of $100 bills banded together in $10,000 stacks. Dan imagined for a moment what he could do with all that money, but he quickly returned to reality and opened the second bag.

The second duffel bag had eight handguns in it, with numerous spare magazines and loose ammunition in the bottom. One was a gold-plated Colt revolver with very intricate engraving along the barrel and cylinder. It was a beautiful piece of art, so much so, that Dan decided he would keep it. He removed it from the bag and tucked it in his waist band.

Dan sat down in the driver's seat next to Luis and chuckled as he thought of his fortunate situation. Not only had he got Luis, but he had enough money to fund his future endeavors indefinitely. Travelling the country searching for these scumbags was expensive and he often worried that he would not have the resources to finish his mission. With the money from the duffel bag, that would no longer be an issue. In addition to that, if Luis disappeared suddenly, and with all that money, the cartel would most likely think he stole it. They would probably put a hit out on him, and the authorities would soon learn of it and be looking for a man on the run as well.

"You know you a dead man, right essay? You know dat. You dead, you family dead, everyone gonna die cause of you." Luis calmly stated as he stared out the windshield at nothing in particular.

Not eager to have his mood spoiled, Dan slapped Luis on the shoulder as he replied, "Sure thing, buddy." They sat in silence for a moment as Luis glared at Dan with a frigid look on his face, and Dan smiled back, almost politely. "Well, let's get going. We're burin' daylight, Luis!"

Transferring Luis to the cab of his pickup went smoothly, although Dan did have to listen to Luis explain, in grotesque detail, how he planned on killing Dan…and his wife…and his children…and pretty much everyone that Dan ever loved. Some of the tortures Luis described were somewhat interesting to Dan. Did people actually do that kind of stuff? Dan imagined, with horror, what it must feel like to be burned alive, or for a person's skin to be peeled off a little at a time! Maybe he should do exactly that to Luis? Seemed fitting, but no. Dan would do things his own way.

Before parting ways with Luis's car, Dan reached into the glove box of his truck and removed a small Gideon's new-testament Bible and a red highlighter. He flipped through the pages until he found the verse he wanted. Luke 17:2. Dan highlighted the verse in red, then wiped it down with a cloth, before placing it in the glove box of Luis's car. Again, a mistake, but one that Dan was committed to doing.

Luis had remained extremely calm and confident since waking, but that would change in a few short hours once they were back at the farm. Taking him back alive was not in Dan's original plan, but it would work out just fine all the same. Luis could scream for days and no one would ever hear him there.

Shortly after being loaded in the truck, Luis chose to take a nap. He rested his head in the corner of the cab, and within a couple of minutes was snoring loudly. He was not worried at all. In his mind, he knew that it was just a matter of time, and he would be free, and the tables would be turned. He knew he would kill Dan at some point, so he might as well rest up until then. Dan looked across the cab when he heard Luis snoring and shook his head in amazement at the lack of concern he exhibited. The man was completely oblivious to the nightmare he was about to enter.

The rumbling of the tires as they crossed the cattle guard in Dan's driveway woke Luis. He peered through the windows as he let out a long yawn. As the two approached the house, Luis inquired about the residence.

"This your place, Homes? Think I'll burn it down too."

Dan had made it home, and there was no need for him to control his anger any longer. At the sound of Luis's voice, Dan grabbed him by the back of the neck and slammed his face into the dash of the pickup. The impact broke the plastic dash into several pieces and appeared to have broken Luis's nose. All the same, Luis laughed as he licked the blood that was running from his nose onto his top lip.

He parked the truck behind the house at the entrance to Rebecca's Garden. Leaving Luis tied up in the cab, Dan retrieved his tractor from the barn and drove to the back corner of the garden to prepare Luis's grave. It only took him 15 minutes or so to complete the task, and it was good that it took no longer since Luis had nearly freed himself by the time Dan returned to him.

At that point, Dan decided to take no chances, and brought a wooden kitchen chair and a roll of duct tape out to the truck. He taped Luis's torso to the back of the chair, his legs to the front legs of the chair, and added tape to his wrist behind the chairback. The sun was beginning to set in the sky as Dan packed the man through the garden and sat him in front of the freshly dug hole. Though he was tired, Dan was committed to finishing the job that night. He brought another wooden chair from the house, along with several work lights, since he knew he would be busy for most of the night. All the while, Luis sat taped to the chair with nothing more than a look of disinterest on his face.

When Dan had completed the necessary setup, he sat down in the chair directly in front of Luis and stared into his dark eyes while he lightly tapped a wooden baseball bat he had brought with him from the house. The sight of the bat did little to stir fear within Luis, but if it would not cause him fear, at least it would bring him pain. Luis was a hardened man. One that did not fear much, or possibly anything, and it showed. The look on his face told Dan he did not fear death, or pain, or anything that Dan could inflict upon him.

Dan sat in silence for a few minutes thinking about that fact. Was this man truly fearless? Would he be capable of making him regret the terrible things he had done? Perhaps not, but nonetheless, he would suffer immense pain, then death, for his crimes. Dan wanted to see him beg for mercy. He wanted to see the fear in the man's eye as he realized his moment of reckoning had come, but he was resigned to the possibility he would be deprived of such.

Dan kicked his chair out of the way as he stood with the bat and said, "This is for my Becky!"

He drew the bat back over the top of his head, and with both hands, as if chopping wood, swung the bat down as hard as he could on the top of Luis's left knee. The loud pop left no doubt bones had been shattered, and from the look of the joint, his lower leg would have fallen off completely if not for the skin keeping it attached. In an instant, Dan realized Luis was not nearly as hard a man as he acted.

Apparently, Luis had been in some form of denial since the beginning of his capture. He had assumed someone would find him, or somehow he would get free, or Dan was simply bluffing, but he had never actually considered he was in true danger. The impact from the baseball bat against the top of his knee not only shattered bone, but also the idea that he was untouchable. He let out a wail so loud, and high pitched that Dan wondered if someone might actually hear him, miles away. Snot ran from his nose as the tears fell from his eyes. He cursed Dan, then begged Dan, then attempted to negotiate with Dan. He claimed he could get Dan more money than he could ever imagine. All, of course, fell on deaf ears, as Dan could not be moved by money, or sympathy, or fear. What he was doing was his only purpose in life, and he would finish or die trying.

It was nearly midnight, and after seeing the tremendous amount of pain Luis was in, Dan decided that he would leave him there to suffer until morning. He wouldn't be going anywhere, and a night of agony was very fitting for that devil of a man. He turned the lights out, and without saying another word, walked back to the barn, and to his bed.

Dan woke the next morning just before sunrise. It was curious to him that he was able to walk to the bathroom and finish brushing his teeth before remembering he had someone to attend to waiting for him in the garden. Indeed, he was awake for 10 minutes before he ever thought of Luis. Coffee and deciding what to eat for breakfast dominated his mind until he noticed the bat in the corner of the room. He picked it up and saw that he had cracked it badly the night before. No worries though, he had two more in the closet.

He made it to Luis just as the sun was breaching the eastern horizon. Luis whimpered loudly when he saw Dan, with the bat across his shoulders approaching. The pain he was experiencing was worse than any he had ever endured. Not only was his knee shattered, it was swollen to four times its normal size. Additionally, the tape around his lower legs had cut the circulation to his feet, and they were swollen so big they did not look human.

When Dan had reached Luis, he drew the bat back like a baseball player, and put all his weight into the swing. The bat landed squarely against the tied hands of Luis, as he screeched with pain. The blow not only made a mess of both his hands, but it broke the back of the chair and flung Luis to the ground face first. Dan grabbed him by the head of the hair and sat him back upright in the chair and laughed slightly at the sight of blood pouring from his nose. Luis no longer looked scary or intimidating. He was a pathetic sight, and Dan was ready to release him.

He was looping the thin piece of rope around the wooden dowel, when suddenly a woman's voice broke the silence. Luis was near unconsciousness, but upon hearing the voice, his eyes widened, and before Dan could stop him, he let out a scream that reminded Dan of a bobcat's scream. Ear piercing, and surely loud enough for the woman to hear.

In a panic, Dan cracked him on the side of the head with the bat hard enough to knock several teeth out, then picked Luis up, chair and all and threw him head-first into the hole he had dug the night before. Had it not been for the chair bottom, Luis would have fell all the way to the bottom. However, the chair was just wide enough to hang on the sides preventing his head from striking the bottom. Luis was 7 feet down the hole, upside down and, for the moment, unconscious.

It was Kelly from the feed store. Dan had asked her to watch Max for a couple of weeks while he was out of town, but he had told her he would be back three days prior. After three days and no word from Dan, she had decided to swing by and check on him before her shift at the store.

"Dan, is that you?" Kelly shouted as she made her way around the side of the house, and towards Rebecca's Garden. She paused for a moment at the entrance, amazed at how beautiful a place Dan had made. She had never seen anything quite so lovely, and the colorful pathways fully lined with flowers lured her inside. As she slowly walked down the path, she again shouted for Dan.

"Daniel, are you here? I've been worried about you. Where are you, Dan?"

Dan frantically shoveled dirt in the hole and over the top of Luis as Kelly's voice drew nearer. All the while cursing himself under his breath for being so stupid.

He had just enough dirt in the hole to cover Luis entirely when Kelly emerged from around the corner and cheerfully chirped, "Oh, hey Dan! I was getting kinda worried about you!"

"I know, I know." Dan said as his voiced cracked slightly. He had never been so nervous in his entire life. If she discovered him, he was done, and as far as he knew, Luis could wake at any moment to tip her off. It was not just the thought of being caught that he was worried about. For Kelly to know what he had done would be overwhelming for Dan. She was a great person, and one of the few people whose opinion mattered to Dan. She thought highly of Dan, and to spoil that perception would devastate him.

He stood leaning against his shovel and staring at the ground as he apologized to Kelly for not phoning her. As he spoke, he noticed, right in front of him, lying on the ground was a bloody tooth that he had knocked out of Luis's head moments earlier. His stomach turned over when he saw it, but with a smoothness he did not know he had, Dan stepped forward and planted his foot on top of it as he threw his arm around Kelly's shoulder and squeezed her.

"I really am sorry, hun. I hope I didn't worry you too much. Let me make it up to you, huh? I'll feed you tomorrow at work. Gonna cook my world famous Boudain Balls tonight, and I'll bring you a few. How's that sound?"

"Sounds great Dan, but I was just worried about you. You want me to bring Max with me tomorrow?"

"Nah, I'll come by and get him tonight. I'm sure he's missing me." He spun her around and patted her shoulder as he led her back through the garden.

"I love this garden, Dan. It's so beautiful! You must have spent forever getting it to look this wonderful!"

"Thanks, Kel. I made it in memory of my daughter, so it means a lot to me. I want it to be special."

"Oh, by-the-way, what was that screech I heard when I pulled up? It scared me so much, I almost left. It almost sounded like…"

Dan cut her off, "Oh, I was digging back there, you know, just prepping the garden, and pulled a muscle in my back. Pain nearly took me to my knees."

"Oh, wow! You ok? That stinks to hurt your back right before going back to work. Tomorrow's probably gonna be hell on ya. Maybe put some ice on it tonight, ok?"

"Sounds good." Dan lied as he rubbed his lower back and grimaced unconvincingly.

"What were you planting back there, anyway? Looked like a big hole. Another tree?"

"Nah, just doing a little fertilizing. Plants need something to keep them growing strong and pretty, ya know."

"Well, alright then. Have fun. Hope your back doesn't bother you too much. See ya tonight." Kelly smiled and climbed in her car as he continued to rub his back.

As she pulled down the drive, Dan fell to a knee and let out a huge sigh of relief. He had almost ruined his entire plan simply by forgetting one tiny detail. One missed phone call. He would have to improve significantly to continue. But for the time being, he needed to bury Luis, who was surely dead by then. He had been upside down in the hole, covered in dirt for the past twenty minutes.

When Kelly was out of sight, he made his way back to the hole and began filling it in. He had not finished the way he intended, but no need crying over an already dead scumbag. He had tossed a couple scoops in the hole, before he heard Luis. That S-O-B was still alive. He could not believe it but started digging him out all the same. When he had uncovered a foot, Dan let down a rope with a slipknot in it and hoisted Luis out of the hole with the bucket on his tractor. After sitting him back up, and cleaning his face off, Dan wasted no time and continued right where he left off.

Luis could no longer talk, as the left side of his jawbone seemed to be broken in two. That whole side of his face drooped significantly and was swollen almost as badly as his feet. He was used up, but conscious, and that is all Dan needed from him. To be conscious enough to listen and understand why he was suffering, and why he would soon die. Luis could not even cry properly he was so mangled, as Dan delivered his condemnation and sentencing. Dan, once again, fashioned his makeshift tourniquet and applied it around the neck of Luis. He turned it slowly and deliberately as Luis began to gasp. Dan sat in front of him and stared into his eyes and watched the life exit Luis. When he had expired, Dan cut him from the chair and tossed him, callously, down the hole once more.

Chapter 9

A Welcome Change

Luis would be Dan's last kill for the year. Though he knew he would need much more than two per year to reach his goal within his lifetime, Dan chose to take a break and focus on better planning for the remainder of the first year. That, as well as Kelly. Though she was only 20 at the time, and more than 10 years his junior, he could not help but grow fond of her. She was very pretty, and not in any sort of superficial way. She was beautiful from the inside out, in a way that was very rare. She needed no makeup or jewelry or fancy clothes to be attractive, she had a natural beauty, and her personality only added to it. Although Dan thought she was beautiful, his attraction to her wasn't really sexual in any way. He just enjoyed being around her, and he seemed to find reasons for doing so more and more often. Sometimes he would pretend to leave town for a few days just so he could stop by to drop Max off.

He loved his job at the feed store, but he was always filled with a bit of disappointment when Kelly was not there. Her company always made the day go by quickly, and she seemed to feel the same way. She was his best friend, maybe his only friend, and by Thanksgiving Dan could tell that Kelly was falling for him too. That realization brought him back to reality, and a very painful reality it was. He knew he could not continue, because to continue would only lead to hurting her. She deserved a happy life, and Dan could never provide that for her. He was tainted, he knew it, and he could not do that to her. He could not abandon his mission, nor could he allow someone else to be dragged into it. There could be no life for them together, so he made up a lie.

In December, Dan confessed to his coworkers, including Kelly, that he had met a woman in a neighboring town and the two were becoming serious. Kelly congratulated Dan, but he could see the hurt in her eyes. She nearly burst into tears in front of everyone before she managed to give Dan a tight hug and step away. It saddened him greatly to see her dejection, but he knew it was for the best. She would move on before long and forget about Dan, and her life would be better for it. And she did, and it was, though she never abandoned or forgot about Dan. The two worked together for years after that day and remained as close of friends as Dan could have ever hoped for. In part, their friendship helped Dan to carry on at times, and it was the only real comfort he had.

By early spring, Dan had created a detailed outline for the entire rest of the year. He had the names of his targets, the dates he would strike, the alias's he would use, places he would stay, he even had alternative targets should one not be possible. He had it all planned. In his second year, Dan would take another eight souls. It averaged out to about one per month, but they were staggered ununiformly. In one instance, he would take a target on the west coast, and six days later strike in New Hampshire. In the month of December, he took three for Rebecca's Garden.

After the third killing, Dan created a journal that he kept hidden in his barn. After each killing, which he referred to in his journal as a "hunt", he would detail the event, critiquing his performance, and logging any revisions to his plan, thus always improving his tactics. The journal was so detailed, there would be no need for a trial should it ever be discovered. It was basically an extremely detailed confession with notes on why he selected each victim, and how he could have done it better. For that reason, Dan took great care to keep it hidden inside the barn.

The term "hunt" evolved from the excuse Dan most commonly used for needing off work, and most of the time, he would incorporate an actual hunt into his trips. Dan Stoker had been on a 7-day Elk hunt in Idaho one year, while Manny Reyes (one of his many alias's) was in Montgomery, AL hunting a much more deserving prey. He enjoyed the solitude of hunting and the beauty of the outdoors, along with the advantage of a very hard to disprove alibi.

His second year was a success by all measures, and along with the invaluable experience he gained, Dan was able to tamp the dirt down on the first of the 10 rows inside Rebecca's Garden. Year two was also encouraging because it confirmed that if Dan kept his current pace, he would be done before his fiftieth birthday. That was a concern from the beginning, that he would become too old and decrepit to finish his work. If he finished at fifty, he would more than likely still be in relatively good health, or so he hoped. Another encouraging sign was that after ten "hunts" there had been exactly zero murder cases opened. Most of Dan's victims were listed on the FBI's wanted list. His plan was working as expected, and year 3 was even more productive than the prior year.

As the years went by, and Rebecca's Garden filled, Dan, almost subconsciously, created a ritual day of remembrance each spring. When the dogwoods were in bloom, he would pick a sunny day and walk the garden, stopping at each tree to view the nametag and remember the demon and why they were there. He would recall their crimes as best he could, and work to convince himself that what he was doing was righteous, that it was a just thing. He had come to think of his victims as "demons", perhaps to help justify his actions in his own mind. To kill a demon could not possibly be a bad thing, and Dan often considered the possibility of demonic possession. It would have certainly explained some of the crimes those men committed. Surely, only a soulless demon could have perpetrated such acts.

By the time he had made it through the garden, he was usually ready to continue. Remembering that much evil tended to spur Dan on. At the end of the garden walk, he would stop outside the garden and rest under the original dogwood in the yard. There he would remember his girls and often sleep and dream of them. On a few occasions, he dreamt that Shelly and Becky urged him to continue, though in reality he supposed that would not have been the case.

Still, he carried on, and for eight straight years the body count climbed. At the end of his first eight years, Dan had put 44 demons in the ground. 44 men, and to Dan's knowledge, not one murder investigation had ever been opened. He had perfected his art. He was 42-years old at the time, and well contented with his progress, but things would soon change for Dan.

It was mid-January, and the weather was especially brutal that year. Along with several inches of snow, old man winter delivered consistent temperatures in the mid-teens and an unrelenting barrage of windstorms that kept Dan and his old friend Max locked down. Dan was relegated to not much more than watching TV and sleeping for nearly two weeks. Max didn't seem to mind though, so long as he got to lay by the fire. He was 14-years old then, and he liked nothing more than to lie at Dan's feet in front of the fireplace. Arthritis had set in a couple of years prior, and Dan feared that he would soon leave him.

Dan was flipping through the channels one afternoon, when a television show caught his attention. Max had been lying in front of Dan, warm and content, but when the narrator began to speak, he decided to push his head up between Dan's legs, so Dan scratched his head while he watched. It was a documentary about a man named Jonathan Ackerman.

Jonathan was a middle-aged man from California who had spent the last 18-years in prison for sodomizing a young boy in his hometown. As soon as Dan heard that bit of information, he was ready to add Jonathan to his list, however, as the narrator continued to speak, Dan's mindset began to change. It seemed that Jonathan had been changed during his time in prison, and he had spent the last 8-years of his incarceration dedicated to assisting victims of pedophilia and child sexual assault, and their families to cope with the trauma. He was a wealthy man and had used most of his fortune for this purpose. The show interviewed dozens of families across the country who had benefited from his foundation, with many of them thanking him personally for his efforts.

"Doesn't matter," Dan thought. "Still deserves to die." He said that part out loud as if attempting to reassure himself. But a seed had been planted inside him, and it kept him up for most of the night. It had not occurred to Dan in the past that there could be some kind of redemption for those demons. That there was a possibility of them having a positive impact on others after what they had done. It bothered him and he tossed and turned throughout the night as he battled with this new idea.

He spent a large part of the next day contemplating this idea. Could it be that God still had a use for the men he considered nothing more than demons? If so, how could he continue? Dan could not know the future, so was it possible that he had prevented one of the 44 from doing something as positive as Jonathan? He paced the floor of the barn for hours as he tormented himself with that thought. According to the documentary, Jonathan's foundation had actually helped in several cases to track down and incarcerate men that were known abusers. The thought that Dan's actions could have even indirectly contributed to the harm of a child was paralyzing.

That night was as sleepless as the one before for Dan. He had made a promise to Becky, had committed himself to fulfilling his task, but Dan was seriously questioning his future for the first time in years. The decision was made for him in the early hours of the morning while he was reading his Bible. Flipping through the New Testament, Dan came across a familiar verse, but one he had put out of his mind years ago. Romans 12:19

"Vengeance is Mine; I will repay, saith the Lord."

He read the verse, then re-read the verse, over and over again as he struggled internally. For a man with 44 murders to his name, his conscious was weighing heavy upon him. Not so much for the act itself, but for the unintended consequences that could have occurred from his actions. Was taking vengeance into his own hands interfering with the plans God Himself had laid out? If so, how could he continue? Who was he to do such a thing?

"Ok...Ok...Ok...I will stop." Dan mumbled to himself slowly as a tear landed on the thin page of his Bible. "It is Yours, not mine."

Dan stood and laid his Bible on his nightstand before walking out into the snow-covered yard. He knelt by the old dogwood tree in front of Rebecca's Garden and wept as he asked for forgiveness. At first to Becky, to forgive him for, among other things, his failure to complete his promise, then to Shelly, and lastly to God Almighty for 44 souls he had taken. He begged, but deep down, Dan felt in his heart that forgiveness would not be granted by any of the three.

He knelt there under the tree for so long that even in 10 degree weather, he fell into a slumber. Something about that old tree did that to him nearly every time he visited. He awoke just before daylight, and half frozen, but feeling much better. He had a wonderful dream there as his body froze to the ground. He could not remember much about the dream, other than the feeling it left him with. The little he could remember was a moment where he was reunited with Becky and Shelly. They were all in the sunlight together, smiling, and happy. He could not remember if they spoke, but Dan knew that he was forgiven, and all was well. They were rare, but he loved dreams such as those. The type that stayed with him for a time even after he had woken. He'd only had a few in his lifetime, but he remembered them all, or at least the feeling they left inside of him. Perhaps that was God's way of sharing a tiny glimpse of Heaven with men.

That was that. Dan's life had been changed in an instant and changed profoundly. The answer was not to take lives but to change lives. If Jonathan Ackerman could help people, then surely Dan could do the same. Dan had collected a small fortune from the 44 men he had slain. Maybe he could use that money as Jonathan had to make a difference, and thus honoring his little girl in a way that she could be proud of. He was resolved to do just that and began almost immediately to do so.

Dan's first action was to anonymously donate tens of thousands of dollars to organizations across the country that assisted the women and children victimized by sexual assault. Each time Dan made such a donation, he could literally feel some of the weight from his own sins being lifted from him. Additionally, he volunteered at a local battered women's shelter where he was able to directly, and positively, affect the lives of dozens of women. Doing those activities brought about a joy within him that he had not felt since Mason Langford. He delighted in the knowledge that he was truly doing something good with his life for the first time in a very long time.

Dan rode that high through the spring and summer, but in early September, sadness once again found him. He had returned home that afternoon to find Max curled up on his bed and breathing raggedly. Dan had known for a while that Max was not in good health, but the sudden change caught him by surprise. Max had seemed fine that morning when he left for work, but by that evening, he was too weak to even raise his head from the bed. Dan scooped him up and headed towards town, calling his veterinarian as he drove.

Dr. Wilson met Dan at the front door as he rushed up the stairs and into the examination room. He gently laid Max down on the cold table and stepped back as the distinct smell of a veterinarian's office filled his nostrils. It was an unmistakable smell, and one that Dan had experienced many times in many different offices, but it was always present and always the same. He had no idea why they smelled that way, and Dan was somewhat confused, even aggravated that his mind would focus on such a thing as his best friend lay in front of him suffering.

Dr. Wilson had known Dan and Max for many years, and he was genuinely saddened to see Max in such a condition. Tears fell from Dan's eyes as Dr. Wilson examined his best friend. He shook his head and mumbled under his breath as he held the stethoscope to Max's chest. It was not a good situation. They both knew it, but Dr. Wilson convinced Dan to leave Max with him overnight so he could be monitored. Dan reluctantly, and regrettably, agreed to go home and return the following morning.

Dan's phone rang at 4am the following morning, with Dr. Wilson delivering the dreaded news. Though he never left his side that night, Dr. Wilson was not able to stop the inevitable. Max had died just a few weeks before his 15th birthday, and Dan was crushed. He sat on the side of his bed and wept unashamed as Dr. Wilson spoke. His best friend was gone.

Dan collected Max later that morning from Dr. Wilson, and buried him in Rebecca's Garden, in the very front, just past the entrance. He had a headstone made for his friend and planted a red rosebush behind his grave. It was a fine resting place for Max, however painful a reminder it was to Dan. Had it not been for his work, Dan would have most likely taken his own life then. However, the new-found joy of helping others sustained him through the second most painful time of his life.

With the exception of losing his best friend, that year was far-and-away the best year of his life since losing his girls. Years prior had been endured through the morbid satisfaction of killing. There was never any happiness in it, but just enough contentment in removing the evil to sustain him. The year of no killing had brought about an actual happiness for Dan. He had met many wonderful people, helped dozens of families, and was for once doing something worth taking pride in. The ladies at the shelter loved Dan too. All of them took a liking to him almost immediately and enjoyed his company tremendously. So much so, that in September, shortly after Max's passing, they surprised Dan with a party at the shelter. It was the nicest thing anyone had done for Dan in nearly a decade, and it almost brought him to tears to see that so many people cared so much for him.

It was late December of that year when Dan's life once again changed drastically. He was working in the kitchen at the women's shelter on that afternoon when he overheard the television in the lobby. At first, he thought he had misheard the reporter, but he threw off his apron and rounded the corner to verify what she was reporting. He must have appeared distraught as he watched the newscast, as the two ladies working with him both stopped by to make sure he was ok.

The hairs on the back of his neck began to tingle as he absorbed what was being said. He could not contain his rage and nearly scared the two women from the room as he shouted at the TV and pounded his fist against the wall. Dan leaned against the wall and tucked his head into his forearm as he repeated, "No, no, no, no, no..."

Alice, one of the ladies helping with kitchen duties, approached Dan cautiously from the side and gently placed her hand inside his.

"Daniel, honey, are you ok? What happened, what's the matter?" She, nor anyone at the shelter had ever see Dan so emotional, and it was somewhat frightening for them to see a man of Dan's size so completely unhinged. She was not scared of Dan, just unsure of the situation and worried for him. Just moments before he was smiling and joking with the women. It was as if a switch had been thrown, and a Dan they had never seen before emerged.

Dan gathered himself and apologized to the two women, hoping earnestly that he had not scared them too much. He had worked with them for the better part of a year and cherished their friendship. Wiping a tear from the corner of his eye, he spoke, asking them to forgive him for his eruption and for needing to leave them short-handed. He needed to be alone. He needed to think.

Chapter 10

The Warpath

Jonathan Ackerman would be number 45. Dan staggered from the women's shelter in a daze as his mind raced and his emotions overwhelmed him. He could not believe he had been so naive. That he had been deceived by the demon that was Jonathan Ackerman. He had swallowed the lie so easily and gullibly that he was as embarrassed as he was enraged.

It seemed that Jonathan was in fact not a changed man. He had just been arrested by the sheriff's department in Los Angeles County for allegedly molesting two children at his foundation. Two children that he was supposedly helping. Two children that Dan could have saved from him. There had been no trial yet, but Dan knew he was guilty, and the hatred he felt for Jonathan was approaching that of Mason Langford himself.

Dan had abandoned his mission, his purpose, for nearly a year based on the lie that a demon such as Jonathan could somehow add value to the world, and that knowledge was turning

Dan's guts inside out. He blamed himself for the pain and suffering of those two children, and potentially many more, that Jonathan had hurt. If he had followed his plan, Jonathan would be in the ground, and those children would not have suffered at his hands.

It was a mistake to have ever stopped. Vengeance was indeed God's, but Dan was the instrument of God, and he would never again stop. Jonathan would pay for his crimes and pay for his deceit.

Dan drove back to his farm, slapping the palm of his hand against the steering wheel ever so often as he silently castigated himself for ever being so naïve. It was near freezing that afternoon, and the drizzle of rain that persisted only added to his gloominess. He stared off into the grey skyline as he turned into his drive. He parked outside his old farmhouse and sat in silence for more than an hour as he continued to blame himself for his inaction.

"Never again." He mumbled as he exited the old truck and turned his collar up. He would take Jonathan, then make up for the wasted year.

The cold wind stung his face as he made his way back to the barn and unlocked the door. He shivered and shook the rain from his jacket, hastily making his way through the door and towards the fireplace. Dan loved a wood fire, and though it was far less convenient than gas logs, he had never entertained the idea of changing. The crackling sounds and familiar scent of a wood fire was therapeutic, and in the winter months, his favorite activity was reading while lounging in front of the flames.

It was not long, and Dan had a comfortable fire blazing inside the fireplace. He rubbed his hands together while he knelt in front of the hearth and warmed himself. Staring into the flames he again lost himself in thought for several minutes.

Sufficiently warmed, Dan stood and walked to his bedroom, where he removed his dust covered journal from a hidden compartment in the wall. It had been a year since he had even looked at the well-worn pad of paper, and he settled into his recliner in front of the fire before flipping to the first page. For several hours, he read, and reread, his entries, which detailed all 44 of his "hunts" and the evolution of his craft. He marveled at the drastic improvements he had made over the years, in planning, in execution, and even in writing. The latter entries, unlike the early ones, were extremely detailed, and read almost like a novel, with the story flowing from page to page. He read the entire journal that evening, and when finished, began a new page.

The following morning was spent researching Jonathan Ackerman. There were volumes of information available on the internet and locating the details Dan needed was a simple task.

Probably due to his wealth, Jonathan was released from jail on bond and was at home awaiting his trial to begin in late April. He was however, required to wear an ankle monitor and not leave his home for the duration of the trial. This was both good and bad for Dan. He would have no trouble finding the man but removing him had become somewhat more difficult.

On a good note, Jonathan, like all the others Dan had selected, lived alone. Dan found it curious that they were all loners, and due to that fact, had become suspicious of any man he met that lived alone. He always considered the worst when he met a grown man without a family, though he knew that his suspicions were irrational. After all, he lived alone, and he would never hurt a child. Dan chuckled to himself as this thought crossed his mind.

"No, Dan. You're a good person. You'd never hurt a child. You've only murdered 44 men. And let's not forget, you let your wife and daughter die! An upstanding citizen you are! Truly a great person!" He shook his head as he sarcastically honored himself. Dan had long since concluded that he was not much better, if at all, than the demons he hunted. He often considered himself nothing more than the resultant evil of such evil, and after seeing Jonathan on the news, he once again fully embraced what he was. Good or evil, it did not matter, Dan had a job to do, and he would see it done.

For Jonathan, Dan planned to use a strategy he had used more than once in the past. He would disable Jonathan's security and internet connection in the early morning hours, then pose as a technician later to gain entry. Most of Dan's victims had perished in their homes, but like Luis, Jonathan was to return to the farm with Dan, alive. He deserved special treatment, and due to his hi-profile status, Dan needed to be as quick as possible inside the house.

Dan was delighted when he saw the location of Jonathan's home for the first time. It was almost the ideal location. The home was nestled on a hillside outside the city, far from neighbors and surrounded by acres of trees. Dan could easily approach the residence undetected, and as far as concerns regarding security systems, he had become near expert level at disabling them.

It was only two weeks from the day Dan saw Jonathan on television to the day he arrived in California. Dan wanted to waste no time, as he thought Jonathan to be more of a flight risk than the authorities did. Once in the area, he spent 4 days surveilling before making his move. Dan watched the house for hours at a time, perched high in a pine tree on the hillside. Jonathan had one visitor per day, and they were there most of the day beginning around 9am. Dan assumed it to be his lawyer, but it did not matter. Only that Dan be gone well before 9am.

A year off had not diminished Dan's skill in the least. He was in and out of Jonathan's residence in under an hour and would have been gone much sooner had it not been for the ankle monitor. Dan had hoped that he would be able to break Jonathan's foot and simply slip the bracelet off, but that turned out to be an impossibility. After incapacitating and restraining Jonathan, Dan attempted to do so, but failed, as the bracelet was too tight to begin with, and Jonathan's foot began swelling immediately once broken.

It was on to plan (b), which took longer, and made quite a mess, but Dan had prepared well for the possibility. After thoroughly prepping his work area, to ensure no evidence would be left, Dan amputated Jonathan's right foot with a surgeon's precision. Jonathan woke briefly during the process, but the sight of the scene was more than he could process, and he passed out shortly after waking.

Dan left the monitor on the kitchen counter, along with a hand-written note from Jonathan, before loading Jonathan and two plastic bags full of bloody evidence into the trunk of his own vehicle. The note proclaimed his innocence and apologized to the people of his foundation for having to leave. He claimed the trial would be a sham and he refused to spend the rest of his life in jail for being framed. Dan had forced him to pen the note prior to restraining him. Before leaving, Dan left the Bible with the highlighted verse in the top of a closet in one of the guest bedrooms. 45 hunts and he had never failed to leave his mark.

The following morning, Dan and Jonathan made it back to the farm. Jonathan had made the long drive crammed into the toolbox of Dan's truck, alongside the bags of evidence. When Dan exited the truck, he heard the faint sound of Jonathan sobbing coming from the toolbox.

"Good. You're not dead!" Dan shouted as he slapped the top of the box. He climbed inside the bed of the truck and opened the top of the box as Jonathan began to beg. He was such a pathetic little man. Frail, and pail skinned with blue eyes that were sunk deep into his face. Dan grabbed him by the pant waist with one hand and the hair of the head with the other and lifted him from the box. He raised him high over his head and dropped him over the side of the truck. Jonathan was hog-tied, with his hands and legs bound together behind his back, so the first part of him to hit the gravel was his chest, and from the sound of things, the impact had broken his sternum.

Jonathan's death was especially brutal and slow. Dan was not only punishing him for his acts of evil against so many innocent children, but he was repaying him for his deceit and lies. For causing Dan to stray from his purpose for an entire year. Long before Dan choked the life from Jonathan, he had begged for death. At least he did until Dan removed his tongue with a box cutter and dropped it down the hole in front of Jonathan. He mercilessly carved the chest and back of Jonathan with the knife until there was no space left. The only reason Dan stopped when he did was because Jonathan was bleeding out. He could not die that way. He had to die by the rope, like all the rest, like they did to his Becky.

Dan returned to the barn naked and soaked in Jonathan's blood. He had stripped all his clothes off there in the garden and buried them with Jonathan, but the blood was still dripping from Dan's hair and onto the concrete floor of the barn. A trail of blood leading from the entrance of the barn to the shower would remain for the rest of Dan's life. He left the trail of perfectly round circles on the floor as a reminder of that day and of his promise to never again stop.

Killing Jonathan merely primed Dan for the bloody years to come. It had set inside Dan a mania, an obsession for killing, that did not subside for the rest of his life. It changed Dan, forever. He no longer took interest in his work in town, at the store or the shelter. Within a year he had quit both and retreated to his farmhouse. He rarely left the farm except to "hunt". His days were spent meticulously planning for his next kill and tending Rebecca's Garden. Her garden was the only thing left in the world that he cared for, and he went to extraordinary lengths and spared no expense to keep it looking beautiful.

Over the next seven years, Dan planted another 52 souls in Rebecca's Garden. Counting Jonathan, he had taken the lives of 96 men by the time he had turned 50-years old. 96 men and

Dan's thirst for blood had not been quenched. He required 100 and would stop at nothing to get them.

Dan was still a hardy man. He had forced himself to stay fit so that he could continue his work. Though nearly 300lbs, he was still slim in the waist and extremely broad in the shoulders. His forearms were huge, and the muscles rippled under his skin when he moved his hands. A short greying beard and a shaved bald head only added to his intimidating presence. Time had aged him no-doubt, but he was indeed, still a very scary man. Years of reclusion had worn away his good nature, and pleasant demeanor, so much so that death and anger were all that was left of him. He was hollow on the inside and hard as iron on the outside. There was nothing left for him in the world, nothing other than finishing. Four more and he could rest.

There were occasions when one of Dan's victims would lead him to another. It had happened a few times in the past, and that is how he stumbled upon William Beckmann. Dan had been surveilling his 96th victim when he recognized William leaving the residence. He recognized his face anyway. He did not know why he knew his face until #96 disclosed his identity in an effort to save himself.

William Beckmann was a very wealthy businessman from Connecticut, and his presence at a low-life's home such as Jack Floyd could only mean one thing. There could be no other reason he would associate with such a man, so Dan knew that Jack was speaking the truth when he said that William was looking for several young girls, 10 or younger, to entertain at a "client's" party in April. This was welcomed news for Dan. He could eliminate

William, then take his final three demons from the party in April. Perhaps he would be done before his 51st birthday.

April was only four months away, so Dan would need to work fast. Being that Jack was completely ignorant to any of the party's details, Dan would need to extract that information from William soon to leave time to plan for his finale.

It was the 3rd of January, and Dan stood leaning on the fence at the entrance to Rebecca's Garden. He stared out across the square lot and noticed how it seemed much smaller than it had 18 years ago when he first returned to the farm. The once wide pathways that separated the rows of sapling dogwoods were much narrower. The trees had grown so large, their branches were mingling and sometimes intertwining with the surrounding trees, creating what would be covered walkways when the leaves returned in the spring. Though the garden was beautiful even during the greyness of winter, Dan looked forward to the spring when it would come to life and its beauty would be on full display.

He stood in silence as the possibility of finally finishing his work comforted him. He imagined how he might spend the remaining years of his life and wondered if he might ever find joy again. Pushing himself from the fence, he sat down under the original dogwood where his mission had begun nearly two decades ago, and once again slept.

The chilling January breeze woke him within the hour, and he was somewhat disappointed to have not dreamt that time. As he drifted off to sleep, he had imagined that he would dream like so many times before. A dream that would show him his path or give him some sort of comfort. However, this time there was nothing, or at least nothing he could remember. Discouraged, he returned to the barn where his old chair awaited him in front of a smoldering fire. He stoked it back to life and sat as he entered #96 into his journal.

The following morning, he began preparing for William Beckmann. He needed to take him by early February to ensure he had enough time to prepare for the party. He needed names, the date, and a sufficient plan to take three souls on the same night. Dan had never attempted something so ambitious, and the worry of the details was weighing heavy on his mind. Finishing his work, only to be discovered by the authorities was not a future he intended on living. Though he wanted to have Rebecca's Garden complete by the end of April, he knew that mistakes could not be afforded. These men were undoubtedly wealthy and affluent. How would he make them disappear without causing suspicion? That was the question he would have to answer before April, but first he would need William.

Unlike the other demons Dan had planted in the garden, William was a "respectable" man. Married, connected, and respected by all in his community. He had no criminal record. He was a good man as far as anyone who knew him would say. It would be hard, if not impossible to make him disappear without concern.

After 96 murders in 17 years, there had never been a single murder investigation opened, or at least none to Dan's knowledge. Dan had managed to persuade the authorities that each one was simply a felon on the run, or perhaps they did not even bother to investigate. Either way, his old method was not compatible with someone like William, who would have no reason to leave his life. No, he would have to be murdered, or kidnapped. There was no way around it this time, so Dan would have to focus on leading the police towards someone else. This "hunt" would require perfection from Dan, and he had but a few weeks to devise a plan.

With a little research, Dan learned that William did in fact have a few enemies. Though he was a seemingly model citizen, there were a few folks in Connecticut that truly hated him. A couple of years prior, William required armed security at his home due to threats made to him and his family from an extremist political group. Apparently, they had threatened to burn his house down when they learned he had donated heavily to Gubernatorial Candidate that was unacceptable to them. The incident did not make national news, but it was serious enough that the State Police stationed officers outside his home for more than two months. Perhaps a disappearance and graffiti with their logo would be enough to steer the authorities away from Dan.

That would be Dan's plan. It was not great, but it could work. Even if the authorities were to rule out the extremists, why would they ever look to Dan? "He" would never be in Connecticut. Dan had no connections whatsoever to William and would be more than thirty hours away when he was taken.

William would be only the third victim taken to the farm alive. It was risky, but not nearly as risky as attempting to torture information from him in his own home. Especially since William was married. Dan would need to be in-and-out, just like with Jonathan. He would also need plenty of time with William to ensure he extracted any and all information he might need. The privacy of his farm was ideal for such work.

With his plan outlined, Dan made travel arrangements and set the date for February 7th. All there was left to do was wait.

Chapter 11

Discovering the Truth

Patience was never one of Dan's virtues, but as he aged his ability to deal with the downtime had all but vanished. It took all he had to keep from heading towards Milford, Connecticut the day he finalized his plan, but his sensibilities won out and he forced himself to remain.

With nothing to do, Dan resorted to one of his few remaining social activities. One that he would have avoided had he been thinking. Thirty miles south of his farm was JJ's Backwoods Bar. Not much more than a rusty shack sitting on a small gravel lot that had been carved out of the surrounding forest. It was a dilapidated place with bars covering each window, of which at least one pane was missing from each and repaired with tape and plastic. Though rundown and uninviting, it often drew a sizeable crowd. It was a rough place with rough patrons, and Dan had been in more than one altercation there over the years. He bore a four-inch scar across the right side of his chest, and a longer one down his upper right arm, given to him by a man who tried to gut him over nothing. Two blood stains on the floor in front of the bar, donated by Dan that night, stood as a reminder to how dangerous of a place JJ's could be.

Dan arrived early Saturday afternoon, with no particular plans for the evening. He thought he may have a couple drinks, or perhaps he would shut the place down. It would be one or the other though. Dan knew that much. Any more than 3 or 4 beers and Dan would be there all night. That's just the way it was with Dan and alcohol, an all or nothing approach.

The parking lot was empty when Dan arrived, but within an hour or so it began to fill. As more and more folks arrived, Dan became less and less inclined to stay. He had downed two beers and 3 shots of bourbon before deciding the atmosphere was not what he needed. The thick cloud of cigarette smoke and the constant yelling coming from the drunk at the end of the bar was wearing on his nerves, so he paid his tab and made for the door. The sun was half hidden behind the horizon as he left the bar, so Dan figured he would just head home and relax for a while before going to bed.

That was not to be though. As Dan was unlocking his truck door, he was struck with a blinding pain in his neck, then unconsciousness. He had not seen anyone in the parking lot as he made his way to his truck, but someone had snuck up from behind and struck him across the back of the head with a short piece of pipe. He knew this because they left the bloody cudgel beside him after they relieved Dan's lifeless body of his wallet. Dan did not wake for nearly an hour, and only after JJ found him lying next to his truck in the gravel. JJ, with the help of two other customers, loaded Dan into his truck and drove him to the hospital after wrapping his head with a somewhat clean bar towel. It took seven stitches to close the gash at the base of Dan's head.

Dan spent the next two days in bed nursing one of the worst headaches he had ever experienced. The incident also convinced Dan to stay away from the bars for a while, as he did not tolerate pain as well as he did when he was a young man. Though his headache subsided on the third day, it was nearly a week before Dan was back to normal, and he took the assault as a sign that he should stay home until he left for Connecticut. It was another week before he left, and rather than drinking the week away, he spent it in his chair reading a novel, then another, and the better part of a third.

He had nearly postponed his visit with William until his stitches were removed, but rather than wait, he bandaged his head and carried on. His biggest fear was that he would somehow reopen the wound in the event of a scuffle and leave his blood at the crime scene. A mistake such as that would surely get him caught, so he was extremely particular in how he wrapped the wound.

The drive was terribly long, and the weather miserable. By the time Dan made it to Connecticut, he was wondering why anyone would want to live through winters such as they had in the Northeast. Everything was grey and dreary, but as he went from town to town, he could not help but notice that the people seemed happy and not bothered by the weather at all.

"I guess you get used to it." He said to himself as he stopped for a waving couple crossing a side street.

William lived on an estate between Fairfield and Milford, Connecticut. Though the home had close neighbors, the 5-acre lot was surrounded by mature White Oak trees and tall hedges that hid the mansion and made the estate more private than Dan had expected. It was a Victorian era 3-story home, built in the late 1830's, though it looked as if it were just built. A beautiful white home with ten large stone columns supporting the front porch that extended the width of the house. Each window was a work of art, with intricate designs carved in their framework. The roof was made of a light reddish tile with a decorative wrought iron fence enclosing it. Just the stone walkway leading to the front of the house was something to behold. Though it had been there since Andrew Jackson was President of the United States, it remained unblemished. It was a sight no doubt, impressive to say the least, to a man who had spent the past two decades living in a small dusty apartment inside an equipment barn.

"The man has it all and still isn't satisfied. He's gotta hurt babies...just babies they are...to be satisfied." Dan mumbled as he stared out the window of the car at the enormous home. A tear rolled down his cheek as he acknowledged," It's evil, Dan. Pure evil. They are all demons, Dan. Never forget that again."

Dan watched the house for nine days before making a move. William's wife left the house that afternoon, and at 2am Dan assumed she would not return that night. An assumption that, unfortunately, turned out to be wrong.

Jack Floyd was a child sex trafficker, and a man that Dan took great satisfaction in destroying. But, along with the satisfaction of ridding the world of such a man, Jack also provided Dan with something else of value. Though Jack knew little of William or the upcoming party, he knew lots related to trafficking and controlling people, and he was more than eager to tell Dan everything. He was an expert, with all the necessary tools to be efficient, and one such tool was Ketamine. He had a medical bag with dozens of prefilled syringes, loaded with enough Ketamine to sedate a grown man for nearly an hour. Delivered intramuscularly, it took effect within a couple of minutes, and would make the long ride back to the farm much more manageable.

Dan took the medical bag with him, along with his usual tool kit, as he crept along the side of the property, using the tall hedges to shield him from the view of William's security cameras. Within minutes, Dan defeated the security system, and entered the home through a basement window. The floors creaked and popped so loudly as Dan made his way to the second-floor bedroom, that he was sure the sounds would wake William. His heart pounded as he slowly turned the brass doorknob and gently pushed the heavy wooden door open. It too attempted to alarm William with its own squeaking. It was a sound fitting for hinges that had been in the home since before the American Civil War.

Enough moonlight had slipped through the window curtain to reveal William's face across the room. He was asleep and snoring faintly. Dan tiptoed across the large bedroom in a useless effort to silence the floors, but it did not matter anyway.

William was dead asleep, sleeping way to peacefully for such a despicable man. How could a man sleep like that with so much on his conscious? Dan stood over him and studied his face for a moment before he covered William's mouth with one hand and injected the Ketamine into his hip with the other. The pressure on his face woke William, and he put up a futile effort to throw Dan from him until the sedative took effect.

With William unconscious on the bed beside him, Dan knelt down and unzipped his tool bag. He removed an older Bible he had purchased from a thrift store some time back and placed it in the top drawer of William's nightstand. As always, Dan highlighted Luke 17:2 in red and wiped his prints from the cover. He then removed a can of orange spray paint from the bag and roughly sketched on the antique hardwood floor, the circular symbol used by the group that so despised William.

After securing William's hands behind his back, Dan threw him across his shoulder and proceeded down the stairway and to the front door. Just as he made it to the base of the stairway, he heard the front door begin to creak. It was William's wife. He dropped William and his bags and rushed forward as he pulled his taser from his back pocket.

As he made it to the door, the lady, half intoxicated, swung the door open wide and looked directly into Dan's eyes. She was terrified, and tried to turn and run, but Dan grabbed her by the hair and dragged he back inside. He tased her across the side of her neck and she collapsed next to her motionless husband. When she saw his face, she whimpered helplessly and closed her eyes, hoping for it all to be a dream.

Dan hurriedly unzipped the medical bag and retrieved another syringe before the lady could get to her feet. He plunged the needle into her buttocks and held his knee across her back until her breathing indicated she had gone under. When he knelt to pick up the small-framed woman, he noticed a small pool of blood on the floor. She had hit her head as she fell from being tased and suffered a small, but bloody cut to her forehead. Dan sighed with a bit of remorse for having harmed the woman. It was the first time in his endeavors that he had ever hurt an innocent, and it bothered him. He gently carried her to another bedroom on the second floor and gingerly placed her head on a pillow. Before leaving her, he bandaged her head and apologized to the comatose lady for his necessary violence.

It was nearly three o'clock in the morning when Dan dropped William into the trunk of his first rental car. He had what he needed, but he was a long way from home, and he would have to transfer William to 4 other vehicles before he made it. It would be a nerve-racking trip for Dan, more so than he even expected.

Early in the drive, Dan realized that stopping every hour or so to give William a dose of sedative was slowing him down tremendously. Rather than doing so, Dan propped William up in the front seat with his hands tied behind him. By doing this, Dan could monitor William and only give him a dose when he absolutely had to. If William began to become sentient, he would administer the medicine, otherwise, he would let him lie. Not only would this be faster, but Dan could better conserve the dwindling supply of sedative. Additionally, Dan did not want to give

William any more of the drug than had to for fear of overdosing him. A dead William was of no use to him.

22 hours of driving, and Dan was spent. He was on the last leg of his trip and wanted to finish but could no longer hold his eyes open. Sleep would be dangerous, but equally necessary. Dan pulled off interstate 44 somewhere near Tulsa and drove for close to an hour before finding a sufficiently private area to rest. He had pulled to the side of a gravel road inside a state park of whose name he could not recall.

It was 2am when Dan leaned across the car and gave William one of his few remaining doses of Ketamine. He planned on sleeping for an hour or so, then dosing William once again before sleeping until daylight. At one point during the trip, William had not stirred for over three hours after a dose, so Dan was fairly sure he would be fine for that amount of time. If he woke, he would wake Dan anyway and he would deal with it. Regardless of the risks though, Dan had to sleep.

He awoke with a jolt as the car door slammed behind William. William had woken just before daylight, and though disoriented, realized the danger he was in. After managing to free his hands from the restraints, William, still not thinking clearheadedly, sprang from the car and took off bare foot through the woods. He must have slammed the door from habit, for if he hadn't, William would have probably escaped Dan. However, that would not be. Dan grabbed a syringe and followed William into the forest. The chase ended abruptly when William lost his footing on a large half-buried rock and rolled his ankle. From the sound of his cries, Dan was sure it to be broken.

Dan leaned against a nearby tree for several seconds taking deep breaths as he tried to recover from the short, but intense chase. William fought Dan off best he could, even cutting him on the side of the face with a small, sharp rock he had picked up, but Dan was simply too much for him. Pinning his head to the forest floor with his knee, Dan sedated William once again.

The walk back through the woods in the dark nearly drove Dan into a fit of rage. Slipping every few feet on rocks, or roots, or fallen timber, and walking face first into no less than a dozen webs of some sort. But it was the briars that caused him to lose self-control. Apparently, he did not return to his vehicle using the path he left from, because at one point he was so thick in a briar bush that he could not move forward. He fought through the tangle of branches and vines as the thorns tore at his arms and legs; though in the end nature won out and Dan had to retreat. The chase through the woods lasted no more than three minutes, though the walk out took Dan closer to thirty, and when he had finally arrived back at the car, he brutishly dropped William next to it and kicked him in the side. Though it was cool outside, Dan was sweating profusely from battling his way through the thickest brush he'd ever witnessed. He was also bleeding steadily from the cut on his face and the stitches on the back of his head. At some point during the incident, he had re-opened the wound and blood was soaking the back of his collar. On top of the two cuts to his head, he was bleeding from both arms and legs from uncountable scratches from thorns. From the looks of the two men, one would have thought that Dan got the worst of it.

That was the last stop before Dan transferred William to the toolbox of his truck and returned the rental. From there it was less than two hours to the farm. He was out of sedative, but he did not care. Dan would let him squirm in the darkness if he woke.

It was early afternoon when the two arrived at the farm, and the sun was shining uncharacteristically bright for a month as typically grey as February. Dan stepped from his truck and looked up to the sun for several seconds, as if to absorb the unexpected warmth and energy it was providing. He felt good, and he was ready to get to work, but William was not cooperating. It had been several hours since his last dose, but he was still unconscious, and it would be another four hours before he was lucid enough to answer Dan's questions.

As Dan waited, he searched the internet for news of the abduction, and was impressed to see it had already made national news. On a good note, the authorities were focusing on members of the political group, but the wife's account of the event were somewhat unnerving. She had told the authorities that she had been sexually assaulted and had provided them with a sketch of the assailant. Though the sketch did not much resemble Dan, she had noted that he had a large bandage on the back of his head. His stomach tied itself in a knot when he heard that detail. Dan paced the floor in his room for several minutes considering this news.

"That could get me caught, Dan. Damn it!"

William's cries for help coming from inside the barn brought Dan back to the present task. Dan had two objectives for his interrogation of William. One, William would confess to Dan his crimes. It would happen or Dan would not end his suffering. Two, William would give Dan every last detail about the party being planned by his cohorts. Those two things had to happen before Dan could send him to Rebecca's Garden.

Dan had laid out a large plastic sheet inside the barn and placed William in the middle of it, strapped to a chair. In front of William was an assortment of tools and blades placed neatly on a table, and a chair for Dan.

William was a respected man, and a man that had a lot to lose, so Dan expected it would take a considerable amount of pain before he laid bare his evil deeds. He had planned for it and was even excited to see how long William would last.

William began screaming hysterically as Dan walked through the barn door and approached. Perhaps it wouldn't take that long after all.

"Who are you yelling to, William? Do you have any idea where you are?" Dan said laughing slightly as he took the seat in front of William. "It's just you and me now, William. No one else for miles. That's why you're not gagged now. It doesn't matter, William. Yell all you want. No one can help you now, William. No one but yourself. You can give me what I require and perhaps save yourself a whole lot of pain, or you can suffer the consequences. It's all up to you, William."

Dan stared patiently at William as he contemplated Dan's statement. Though it was cool inside the barn, beads of sweat were running down the sides of William's face, and his shirt collar was visibly wet from both sweat and tears. His cries faded as he attempted to regain his composure. He sat quietly for a moment taking deep and rapid breaths as he studied Dan. William could not recall ever seeing such a hardened and rough looking individual. Sitting on the small wooden chair made Dan look even larger than he was, and the scars across his face and arms told William that he was a man who had seen much violence in his lifetime.

William was absolutely terrified by the sight of Dan, but he managed to squeak out a trembling reply.

"Wh..What do you want with me...?"

Dan smiled as he leapt to his feet and gave William a friendly slap on the shoulder. He paced around William as he spoke, and William frantically tried to watch him each time he moved beyond his view.

"Glad you asked, William. All I want from you is information. Let's do this the easy way though, ok? I don't want to have to hurt you to get what I need, but I promise you, William, I will if need be. Ok? So...First things first. What were you doing at Jack Floyd's home? And before you answer...you should know this. I asked Jack the same thing, but he lied. He lied, William, and I bet you can't guess what happened to him?"

Dan paused in front of William and waited for a response. "No? No guess? Ok, well...I'll tell you. Jack is buried in the garden just right over there." He pointed across the barn towards Rebecca's Garden and stared intensely into William's eyes. From the look of terror on his face, Dan thought he would probably give him everything without having to lay a finger on him. William was a coward like all the other men Dan had taken, and preserving himself would be his only objective.

"I...I..." William hesitated for a moment as he thought. He was fairly sure that Dan knew what he was doing, but he did not want to take the fall for Victor. "I was getting girls for Victor.

Victor Berghoff. You know him? He's sick, but I had to you see. He required six young girls, and I must do what Victor says. You don't understand. I had to."

Dan cut him off, "Good, William. See that wasn't so bad, was it? I believe you, William, but right now, let's just keep your answers short so we aren't here all night. So, this Victor Berghoff needed six young girls for what?"

"A party…"

"Ok, stop there. What kind of party William?"

"You know what kind…" William replied as he dropped his head.

"Yeah, I thought so, William. When is this party?"

"It's in April, the Week of the Derby."

"What Derby?"

"Kentucky."

"And where will it be, William?"

"At his place. In Lexington. Victor's. Please let me go now!" William's voice cracked as he begged for his release.

"Not just yet, William. I'll need the address and the exact date, buddy." Without raising his head, William nodded.

"Good, now who's gonna be at this party, William? I want names." Dan reached down and grabbed William by the chin so he could look him in the eyes.

"We were all invited. Maybe 10 or 12 of us."

"Names, William!" Dan raised his voice as he tightened his grip on William's chin.

"Ok, Ok…let me think…let's see, there's uh, Victor and Robert Newberry and Governor Willet…and ummm…Senator Langford…and.."

"Senator Langford?!? What do you mean? Why would he be there?" Dan's eyes were wide open and glaring violently at William. "You liar…I'll smash your face…"

"No…I swear it…Senator Langford…Marvin Langford. It's his party. He has Victor plan it every year. I swear to you!"

Dan sat back down in his chair and dropped his head as he absorbed what William had just told him. It could not be. Marvin was a good man. He probably saved Dan's life all those years ago. William was lying!

"You lie…" Dan looked up and grabbed William's collar, pulling him close. "You lie, William!" Dan repeated yelling into the frightened man's face. He did not want to believe it, but Dan knew it was true just from the helpless look on William's face. Both men were weeping as Dan released William and again dropped his head in thought.

"Prove it. Prove it or you die now!" Dan grabbed a hammer from the table to his side and raised it above his head.

"I can't…ummm, wait…please…please!!!! Just let me think. Please!!! I swear it's true…just…" William bowed his head and closed his eyes tightly, expecting the hammer to drop.

"You will prove it, William! So help me God, or your brains will be all over this floor!!"

"Ok, please!!! Just give me a minute…let me think…he's a US Senator for God's sake!!! He doesn't allow for proof…there is no eviden…" William's mind flashed back to several years prior. He was with Victor following one of their parties and the two were extremely drunk. Victor was telling stories of his earlier exploits and mentioned one involving Senator Langford. Some years back, Senator Langford, with Victor's assistance, had raped and murdered a young girl from Marvin's hometown. It was long before he had become a Senator, long before he had sophisticated his methods. It was a girl whom him and his stepson had taken turns with for nearly two days before strangling her. Victor arrived on the second day to join and document the experience.

As William told the story to Dan, Dan fell to his knees and wept uncontrollably, tearing his shirt from his chest as he agonized. It could not be! It could not!! William was describing his Becky! Dan's mind was shattering right in front of William, so much so that William felt some sort of pity for his captor. William sat silent as he watched Dan in confusion. Why had that story caused him so much pain?

After several minutes of writhing on the floor, Dan again stood, only this time with a maniacal scowl on his face. "You will prove what you have just claimed, or I will rip your fucking head off with my bare hands, you sick fuck!!" Dan grabbed him by the throat so hard he nearly broke his neck. William was trying desperately to say something, so Dan reluctantly eased his grip.

William gasped for air as he exclaimed, "Pictures...Victor has pictures...I've seen them!!! He has them I swear!!! He said he kept them because Senator Langford liked to look at them from time to time. I've seen them. It's proof for sure. They would send the Senator to prison forever if they were ever found. Terrible pictures. Of the two men with the girl...even after they had killed her..."

Dan released his grip on William and left the barn. He went to his favorite spot under the dogwood and cried until he could not any longer. It was more than an hour before he returned to the barn. He had to clear his mind. He needed to think straight before continuing with William. Dan had to be sure that he had every last detail from William before burying him, and he could not do that while imagining the scene William had just described. Passing by William with not so much as a glance in his direction, Dan went to his room and laid on his bed. It was late in the evening and the news Dan had just received had drained every last drop of energy from him, so he decided to rest until morning before continuing. He went back in the barn to gag and properly secure William for the night before returning to bed.

William awoke the next morning with a painful slap across the face from Dan.

"Wake up you fucking worm!" It took but a moment for William to remember the nightmare he was in. Dan was standing over him shirtless and breathing heavily, like a bull inside the cage at a rodeo. He was angry, much angrier than William had witnessed prior. William timidly looked up at the giant as the tears began to flow once more.

Dan stretched out his arm and shoved the four tiny black and white photos of him and Becky into the face of William. "Is this the girl?" He asked with a voice quivering with rage.

William's face went pale when he saw the photos. Dan knew by the look on William's face that it was his Becky, but he waited for an answer all the same. William dropped his head once again and begged for mercy as he confirmed what Dan already knew.

In his opposite hand, Dan held the tourniquet. The rope had been replaced many times over the years, but the short wooden dowel was the one from the beginning. The ends were rounded and smooth from years of use, and the center of the dowel was shiny and grooved from the force and friction of the rope. William never saw it until it was around his neck and tightening. Dan had planned to force a confession from William before his death, but what he had already said was confession enough.

"My Becky's death was entertainment to you, you bastard! Did you enjoy seeing her there in torment? Did you?? I can see you laughing as you stared at the pictures of my broken baby girl. You and Victor will die for that! She was my world and the likes of you STOLE her from me!!!" He shouted louder and louder as he tightened the rope. Dan twisted the rope tighter than he had ever, so tight that had the rope been strong enough, it might have severed William's head. He twisted and twisted until Williams eyes bulged from his purple head, then twisted more. He did not stop until the rope snapped like a rubber band. When it broke, though the man was already gone, Dan continued to squeeze him by the neck with his hands as he cursed him.

Marvin Langford was the Devil that had haunted Dan's dreams for nearly two decades. He had taken both of Dan's girls and deceived him along the way. Dan had actually hugged his baby's killer and thanked him just days after her death. For almost 20-years Dan believed he owed his daughter's murderer a debt of gratitude. It was beyond sickening to Dan and he would have his vengeance. At all costs, no matter the consequences, Marvin Langford would die by Dan's hand.

Chapter 12

Agent Jennings

Special Agent Jennings sat staring at the old Bible on her desk while tapping its faded leather cover with her finger. It had been two months since the disappearance of William Beckmann and the trail had gone cold. None of her leads had turned up fresh evidence, and the only thing she had to go on, other than a vague description provided by Mrs. Beckmann, was the Bible that lay in front of her. There was nothing significant about it, no defining features that stood out, just an old King James Bible. However, Mrs. Beckmann swore it did not belong to William and was insistent that it had been left there by his abductor. She brought it to Agent Jennings a day earlier after noticing it lying in the top drawer of her husband's nightstand. Jennings had it dusted immediately, but the only prints found were those belonging to Mrs. Beckmann.

"What is your significance? Why were you left behind? Were you really left behind?" Jennings mumbled to herself as she picked up the Bible and started flipping through its pages aimlessly. If it were in fact left at the home by the perp, there had to be some purpose. The mystery of the Bible intrigued Agent Jennings, and it was a mystery she had to solve.

She slammed the book closed between her hands, and as she did, Casey caught a glimpse of the red. Her green eyes widened, and an uncomfortable knot formed in her stomach as she frantically reopened the pages in search of the mark. She had missed it before, but there, in the third book of the New Testament, she found a single verse highlighted in red.

The verse meant nothing to her, but the fact that it was marked was important. Perhaps the book was left by the perpetrator, and more importantly, perhaps he left his fingerprint on the pages! The outside and inside of the covers had been dusted, but not all 1200 pages. She rushed the Bible back down to forensics and sat impatiently at her desk biting at her thumbnail until the results were delivered to her.

Casey Jennings was a 10-year veteran of the FBI, who had joined shortly after serving 8-years as a US Army Officer. Athletic and extremely driven, she had always been a top performer, and she loved more than anything to catch the bad guy. Though a good agent, Casey was a loner, and a woman that had a strong aversion and distrust towards men. This, in part, from her experiences in the military, but more so from the abuse she suffered as a child. She was a product of the foster system, or rather an unfortunate victim. She could not remember her biological parents. They both died while she was very young, but she remembered vividly the multiple men who made her life a living hell for years. Men who were entrusted with her, to care for her and protect her, were the same men who drove her to attempt suicide at 16-years old. She still had the scars on both wrists to remind her of that terrible period of her life.

She lived alone in an apartment in New Haven, Connecticut and had virtually no life outside of work. She pretended it was due to her workload, but the truth was, she would simply rather work than play. She spent most of her spare time at the gym, or at home reading, and she liked it that way.

Though she was not a large woman, Casey was extremely fit, and more than capable of subduing most any man. On many occasions she had arrested men twice her size, though they resisted like hell. Two years prior she was suspended for a month after breaking a man's nose during an arrest. He had resisted, and nearly broke Casey's arm, but the problem was, she kicked him after he was cuffed. It was the only time in her professional career that she had lost control, but the promises from the man to rape her to death were more than she cared to hear.

A rush of adrenaline ran through her when she learned they lifted several prints from the pages of the bible. One was Dan's right thumb print at the bottom of the highlighted page, but there were several others found throughout the Bible belonging to others. Before any matches were even made, Casey somehow knew the one on the bottom of that page belonged to William's abductor. It was a gut feeling, but one she would have bet her life on. All the other prints were of no concern to her.

A short time later, and the lab had matched the print to one of Dan's. There were prints from three other unknown individuals, but again, that did not concern Casey. Dan's prints were on file with the ATF from purchasing a suppressor some 25-years ago, and Casey wasted no time taking the news to her supervisor. It was a solid lead, one that needed to be pursued, but Casey wanted an arrest warrant issued for Dan right away. However, her supervisor was not as convinced as Casey that a fingerprint found in a 40-year-old Bible was any proof at all, let alone enough to arrest a man on. Especially since Dan was a farmer on the other side of the country with no apparent ties to their victim, and there were at least three others who had handled the same book.

"Is this the man you saw in your home, Mrs. Beckmann?" Casey held up the mug shot of Dan from 18 years prior and rapidly tapped her foot on the floor as she waited for her response. In the photo, Dan's face was thin, and pale, and his eyes looked as if they were sunk too far into his skull. A head full of thick black hair, and a clean-shaven face, was completely different from what Mrs. Beckmann recalled. She remembered a giant of a man, completely bald with a thick, full face and a beard speckled with grey.

"That's not him, hun." It was true, the photo looked nothing at all like Dan. He had nearly drank himself to death during that period of his life, and he was practically unrecognizable from the 50-year-old Daniel Stoker. A more recent photo would have doomed Dan, but at the time, the old mugshot was all Agent Jennings had available.

"I need you to be sure, Mrs. Beckmann. This photo is 20-years old." The agitation in Casey's voice was unignorable, and the tapping of her foot became louder and faster. She knew it was Dan. She just needed Mrs. Beckmann to remember.

"I'm sorry Agent Jennings. I really am, but the man I saw looked nothing like that. I wish it were him. I really do. I would do anything to get my William back, but…" Her voice tapered off as her mind began contemplating the possibility that her husband was probably dead. Mrs. Beckmann bit her bottom lip as she attempted to hold back her tears, but her emotions were overwhelming her.

Disappointed and angry, but unswayed, Casey thanked the grieving woman and returned to the field office. She needed to convince her supervisor to allow her to go and talk with Dan even though Mrs. Beckmann had just stated conclusively that he was not the one. She knew that if she found him, she would discover the truth and have the case closed within a week. Though he truly believed it to be a waste of time, Agent Timmons granted her permission, mainly due to mounting pressure being applied for him to solve the case. William was a prominent individual with lots of friends in high places, and someone like him just vanishing had a lot of very important people very nervous.

As Casey packed her bags that afternoon, Dan made his way across western Oklahoma with Victor's body. Marvin Langford was due to be in Lexington in two days, so Dan would have to hurry if he was to beat him there. He knew it was likely that he would never again have an opportunity to take Marvin and choking the life from him was the only thing left in the world that Dan wanted.

The long drive home provided Dan plenty of time to think about the past, as well as the future, and to remember of how Marvin had destroyed his life. The five polaroid pictures of his daughter and her killers lay face down in the seat beside him. Seeing those pictures nearly killed Dan. The thought of his daughter's pain and fear had tormented him for years, but nothing like what he felt when he saw those images. For the first time, he had seen with his own eyes the horror of what she went through and the look of absolute hopelessness in her eyes. The photo with the bloody fingerprint was the most horrifying image he had ever seen, and it was proof that Marvin Langford was beyond a monster. He was the Devil. The cold smile on his face, and the look of complete satisfaction in his eyes as he posed with Becky's lifeless body, was not human.

Dan did not wish to live anymore. He was ready for the pain, sadness and anger to be gone even if it meant his soul would be destroyed in hell. He was ready to go, but not before he sent Marvin there first. Dan prayed repeatedly on his way home that God would allow him to have his vengeance. Just let him have Marvin and he would pay any price.

Dan wasted no time once he made it home. He had to bury Victor that night and gather everything he would need for his return trip to Kentucky. If he hurried, he could get a few hours of sleep. By leaving in the morning, he could be in Lexington by midnight. According to Victor, Marvin would arrive the following morning, which was a full day before any of the other guests. Dan would have 24 hours alone with Marvin, and he planned to use every minute of it.

Victor saw to it that Dan got minimal rest that night. His fat body was much too large to fit down the hole dug by the tractor, so Dan spent two hours in the middle of the night widening the hole. The hole had to be widened so much, that at one point Dan considered using a chainsaw to get Victor down it. Had he done so it would have been much easier on his back.

Returning to the barn well after midnight, Dan sat down in his chair and logged Victor into his journal as number 98. The old book was more than two inches thick and coming apart at the seams. Its pages filled with the details of 98 murders as well as Dan's reasoning for taking each man. Dan filled several pages with the events of the past couple of days and continued writing for over two hours before falling asleep in his chair with the journal still laid across his lap.

Dan woke just as the sun was topping the tree line east of his farm. Though he had only slept for a few hours, he was refreshed and ready to get moving. He laid the journal on a pillow in the center of his bed, almost as if to display it, before exiting the barn to load his gear in the truck. Halfway down the drive he remembered the revolver in his dresser drawer. On most of his "hunts" throughout the years he did not take a firearm with him, but this time, for Marvin, he would take no chances. Marvin would die the following day one way or another. Dan swore it as he grabbed the gold-plated revolver from the drawer and tucked it in his waistband behind his back. Seeing the fancy revolver again reminded him of Luis from so many years ago. He recalled how, at the time, he concluded that there could not have been a more despicable man alive than Luis. The years had proven Dan wrong.

He had almost made it back to his truck when he heard the familiar sound of tires passing over the cattle guard at the end of his drive. Squinting his eyes, he could make out a black SUV through the cloud of dust rising from the gravel. Dan grew nervous as the vehicle approached. He feared the worst. That he had been caught, and they would attempt to arrest him before he could get to Marvin. He ran through several scenarios in his mind as he waited on his uninvited guests and determined that he would not allow anyone to detain him. Dan had never killed an innocent before, but he resolved in his mind that morning that he would do so if needed. Nothing short of dying would keep him from Marvin Langford.

Special Agent Jennings pulled in behind Dan's truck and stopped as a cloud of dust engulfed her vehicle. She sat staring at Dan from behind mirrored glasses as he leaned against the side of his truck and stared back. She waited until the dust settled before exiting and greeting Dan with a smile.

"Good morning!" She said loudly as she approached Dan.

"Morning." His reply was less friendly. Dan remained perched against the side of the truck as Casey made her way to the other side of the Dan's truck. She too leaned against the bed as the two faced each other and talked.

"Special Agent Jennings, FBI. I'm needing to speak with Daniel Stoker please."

"You got him. What brings you out here, ma'am?" Dan spoke slow and impressively calm considering he was on the verge of a nervous breakdown. "Damn it! Why did it have to be a woman!" He complained to himself as he wrestled with the notion that he may have to kill her.

"Going somewhere, Mr. Stoker?" Casey asked as she studied the bags loaded in the bed of the truck.

"Yes ma'am. Headed to…Kentucky." He hesitated as his mind fabricated a story. "Was about to leave when I saw you pull in. Got a fishing trip planned at Lake Barkley."

They both stood in awkward silence for several moments as the two studied one another. Casey knew Dan took William. She knew before she left Connecticut, she just had no proof. Dan knew she knew something and was waiting to see if he would have to draw his weapon. He lowered his right hand to his waistline and rested his palm on the grip of the pistol.

"You ever been to Connecticut, Mr. Stoker?"

Dan paused for a moment before clearing his throat to respond.

"Can't say that I have. Why do you ask?"

"Do you know a man by the name William Beckmann?"

His stomach fluttered as he contemplated drawing on her. "Doesn't ring a bell. What's this all about Agent…"

"Jennings. Special Agent Jennings. Mr. Stoker could you tell me why your fingerprint would be on a Bible inside a man's home all the way up in Connecticut?"

"Do what?" He tried to look surprised, but Dan was sure he just looked silly. "A Bible, you say? Why would you drive across the country to ask me about a fingerprint in a Bible? That doesn't sound like something the FBI would be interested in. Is it a stolen Bible or something?" Dan chuckled insincerely at his question.

"Mr. Stoker, William Beckmann was abducted two months ago, and the only piece of evidence left at the scene was a Bible. A Bible with your fingerprint in it, and I find that highly unusual." Agent Jennings spoke as she slowly made her way around the back of the truck. As she rounded the side of the truck, Dan turned to face her. When Dan stood and looked down at her, for the first time, Casey realized just how massive he was. A lump developed in her throat as she envisioned herself attempting to restrain him. She was alone, and miles from any help, and for the first time in a very long time, a bit of fear entered into her mind.

"Ma'am I couldn't say for sure." His mind raced for an answer. Any answer that could be plausible would do. Anything to get her out of there. She could come back later, that would be fine, but she couldn't stop him now. He couldn't let her. He owed that much to his Becky, but the thought of killing Casey was nauseating to him.

Casey was about to speak when Dan stumbled his way through a possibility. "Well, I do like to shop at thrift stores. Perhaps I once looked at the same Bible as that William guy? I don't know? You know, I've always been kind of a collector of Bibles. Especially the older ones. They remind me of my younger days. I guess I must have picked that one up somewhere at some time. Never been in Connecticut though, and for sure didn't take some man I've never even heard of!"

Dan tried to look offended by her insinuations, but he was more impressed that she'd discovered him than anything. 17 years of murder, 98 Bibles left, and she was the only one to have ever figured it out. The look on Casey's face told Dan that she knew he was lying, and he silently prayed that she would just leave. Just leave and let him finish.

"Right. Perhaps." She was not convinced at all, but she was not prepared to attempt to detain him. Especially since she was alone in the middle of nowhere, and Dan looked like an actual giant standing in front of her. The scars on his arms and face told Casey he was a brawler, so she relented.

"Well, Mr. Stoker. I won't keep you now, but I may have some further questions for you in the coming days. Do you have a cell phone where I could contact you?"

"Sorry Ma'am. I have no phones. Kind of like it that way too. Now if you don't mind, I'm going to get on my way. Got a fish waiting on me to catch him in Kentucky. Good luck with your investigation." Dan said as he turned and opened the door to his truck. He sat down and closed the door as Agent Jennings walked to the window and leaned in.

"Oh, one other thing, Mr. Stoker. Does the verse Luke 17:2 mean anything to you?"

Dan turned to her and stared fiercely into her eyes. A look of resolute anger emerged on his face as he spoke.

"It does ma'am. Like all the other verses inside the covers, it should mean something to every man. But that one in particular? Sure. I've known that one since I was a kid."

"I read it, Mr. Stoker, but I couldn't make any sense of it. What does it mean?"

"To me? It's simple. I'd say it means that anyone who would harm a child would, in the end, prefer being drown in the depths of the sea rather than suffer the vengeance that awaits them from God Almighty. Now, good day to you." He left Agent

Jennings standing in a cloud of grey dust as he pulled away and headed towards the road.

Casey had investigated Dan's past on her way to his homestead, and she knew of the circumstances surrounding his wife and daughter's death. When she heard his explanation of the verse, she realized how it could mean so much to him, however, she couldn't fit William in to the picture. Rebecca's assailant committed suicide nearly two decades ago. She stood in his drive for a moment reflecting before following Dan down the drive and onto the dusty gravel road. There had to be a connection, she just needed to keep looking.

As Agent Jennings followed behind Dan, she suddenly realized something was very off regarding his alleged trip. A fishing trip to Kentucky? He indeed had quite a bit of gear crammed into the bed of his truck. He was definitely going on a long trip, but of all the gear he had, there were no poles, no tackle, no bait, no boxes. He literally had nothing in his truck to indicate he was going fishing.

"If you're not going fishing, Daniel, where are you going?" Perhaps he knew they were closing in on him? Was he going to run? Casey did not know what Dan was planning, but she was going to find out. Even if it meant following him all the way to Kentucky.

Chapter 13

A Reckoning

He knew she was following him. Though they had not even made it into town, Dan knew what she was doing. Agent Jennings was going to be a problem for Dan, and a problem that he would rather deal with sooner than later.

He sped up, leaving her choking in the dust from the road. Within a few moments, she had slowed down, and he was out of her sight. A couple miles up the road, Dan slammed his brake pedal to the floor as he passed Murphy's Feedlot. He had an idea.

There were at least 50 head of cattle in the small lot just off the left side of the road, and no one around to interfere with him. He jumped from his truck and bolted towards the 16-foot gate at the entrance to the lot. Swinging it open wide, he rushed inside the lot and began pushing the steers towards the gate.

He had to work fast if it were to work. Agent Jennings was just a mile or so behind him, and she would be there any moment. Dan was screaming and clapping his hands wildly as he ran from the back of the lot forward, leading the steers through the gate and into the roadway. They would not delay Agent Jennings for long, but perhaps long enough for Dan to ditch her.

It took no more than thirty seconds, and the old gravel road was completely blocked by the 800-pound animals. She would have a time trying to maneuver her way through that wall of hooves and horns. An eruption of dust spewed across the road as Dan pressed on the gas pedal and sped away. Visibility on the road had already been obscured by the haze, but after Dan took off, the 50 head of cattle all but disappeared in the brown cloud.

Casey cruised down the roadway, unconcerned when Dan accelerated. He was leaving a trail a blind man could follow, so being a mile or two in front of her would not matter. She drove through the brown haze as she considered what Dan might be planning. Dan seemed genuinely surprised to see her at his farm, and she was certain the fishing trip story was made up spontaneously, so she wagered that he was truly going to Kentucky. Just not to fish.

She could not have been travelling more than 35 miles per hour when she hit it, but to Casey, it felt like she had run into a brick wall at twice that speed. She had been admiring the small field to the left of her, filled with petite yellow flowers, or perhaps weeds of some type. Whatever they were, they seemed beautiful to her as they swayed with the wind. That was the last thing she remembered seeing before plowing through the backside of a steer and running off into the ditch to the right of the road.

She was immediately sore, but thanks to her seatbelt and a properly functioning airbag, she was unharmed, though the same could not be said for her rental vehicle or the steer. Not only did it feel like it, but the front end of the SUV looked like it had run into a brick wall. The front quarter of the vehicle had vanished, and both front tires were flattened. The steer lie dead in the ditch maybe 20 yards ahead of the vehicle.

"Nice, Dan. Not bad." Agent Jennings knew it was the work of Dan, but was still unshaken, as she had a backup plan. He could not escape her. She had been at it for too long to let a perp she was certain to be guilty just up and vanish.

Casey sighed deeply as she walked past the deceased animal and made her way down the road searching for adequate cell phone signal. The possibility of having to walk the 15 miles back to town was not a welcome one, especially with the high-heeled shoes she chose to wear that morning. In the end, she walked almost 2 miles before being able to call for a tow truck. All said, Dan's cattle trap put him four hours ahead of Casey, though Dan believed he had lost her altogether. Undeterred, Agent Jennings procured another rental and headed east.

He knew he had lost her, but Dan was sure Agent Jennings would be looking for his truck, possibly even using local and state law enforcement to track him. To ensure she would not further interfere with his plans, he rented a vehicle under one of his aliases just outside of Little Rock, Arkansas. It would take her days to find him if she found him at all. Either way, he would have enough time for Marvin, and that's all he was concerned with.

As planned, Dan arrived at the Lexington mansion around midnight. He pulled the rental car down the long drive and parked it in one of the six bays on the large stone garage behind the home. All that was left was the wait, which had always been Dan's least favorite part. He was exhausted from two days of driving, and he desperately needed to sleep before morning, but his nerves would not allow it. So, instead of sleep he spent two hours preparing the basement for Marvin's arrival.

Nearly 20 years ago, Dan had given up on ever finding true justice for his daughter, but that all changed when he met William Beckmann. Thanks to William's information, it was but a matter of hours, and he would finally have his vengeance. In a few short hours, he would look into the eyes of the man who, not only, killed his daughter, but also his wife, and all that was good inside of Dan. Dan would soon have the justice he had longed for and the closure he needed. Before the day was done, Marvin Langford would witness the monster he had created, and he would truly wish that a millstone had been tied to his neck and him cast into the sea.

Dan laid on the sofa in the basement as he stared at the ceiling and contemplated what was about to unfold. Scenario after scenario ran through his mind, but none seemed painful enough or quite fitting for Marvin. His imagination went from skinning him alive, to impaling him on a pike, to crucifying him, to simply shooting him in the face as soon as he opened the door. None of it was enough, but perhaps Dan could not provide enough punishment for such evil. Nevertheless, he would try, and he would have plenty of time alone with Marvin to do so.

Agent Jennings pulled into the gas station parking lot almost 4 hours after Dan abandoned his truck. Reaching under the rear passenger side wheel-well, she removed the small tracking device she had installed that morning at farm.

"Where you at, Daniel?" She whispered as she looked around the parking lot. "Where you going?"

It took an hour of interviewing bystanders for her to learn that Dan had called a cab from the payphone outside the store. Another hour or so, and she had located the driver and learned he was dropped off at a local auto rental. By the time Agent Jennings was able to access the onboard GPS from the rental, Dan was only a couple of hours from Lexington. Casey's agitation for being more than 8 hours behind him was very plain to see.

Dan eventually made it to sleep, and he nearly slept too long. The unmistakable and unyielding chime of the doorbell woke him promptly at 7:30am. Grabbing his taser in one hand, and the revolver in the other, he rushed up the stairs towards the sound, cursing himself the whole way for not being better prepared for Marvin's arrival. An uneasiness grew as he approached the door. He could see the silhouette through the stained glass door standing motionless. The doorbell rang again as Dan swung the door open and shoved the golden barrel of the revolver between the eyes of the unsuspecting man. The boxes held in his hands fell to the ground in front of Dan as he frantically backed away, stumbling down the stairs as he went.

Dan sat the gun on the porch and holding his hands above his head followed the man down the stairs towards the van apologizing emphatically for the misunderstanding. It did no good. The man was completely overcome with fear, and once back to his feet, returned to his van with a sprinter's speed. He was down the driveway and out of sight in a matter of seconds. Dan sat on the bottom step of the stone stairway, shaking his head in disapproval for nearly scaring the life out of the deliveryman. He sat for several minutes in regretful reflection before returning to the house and to his business at hand.

At 8:30am, the doorbell chimed once again. This time it was the visitor Dan had been waiting for, and this time he was prepared. There was no uneasiness in Dan this time. No nervousness or anxiety. Only anger. He could not identify Marvin through the stained glass on the door, but he knew it was him. Marvin stood outside ringing the doorbell continuously and cursing at Victor to hurry up as Dan approached. 20 years and he would finally have his daughter's killer and he was relishing that fact.

Dan tucked the revolver in his waistline and casually opened the door. Marvin's rantings ceased abruptly when he looked up and saw a very different Daniel Stoker than he remembered from so long ago. The color in Marvin's face disappeared as he tried to understand the situation he had just entered. Dan thought he might attempt to run until Marvin broke the silence with a forced friendliness.

"Dan? Daniel Stoker, is that you? What on earth are you doing here? Haven't seen you in…how long's it been, friend? You doing ok?" His voice was calm and sincere, and if it weren't for the things Dan already knew, one might have thought Marvin was happy to see Dan. Marvin was a professional liar, by necessity, and a damn good one. He had fooled many people, for many years, including Dan.

He slapped Dan on the shoulder as he crossed the threshold into the mansion. Marvin was unsure of the situation but continued as if there was some reasonable explanation for Dan's presence.

"So, Daniel, what's going on? Where's Victor?" Marvin said as he put on his best fake smile and pulled his cell phone from his pocket. He was in process of calling Victor when Dan, walking towards him, reached into the front pocket of his shirt and retrieved the bloody polaroid picture of Marvin with his daughter's corpse.

Marvin's eyes grew wide when he saw what Dan had discovered and attempted to run past him and out the front door. He was stopped painfully when Dan grabbed a handful of his greying hair and slammed him onto the tile floor. Still there was no expression on his face.

"Now wait a minute, Dan! I'm a US Senator for God's sake! What are you doing? Have you lost your mind, son? That's not me in that picture. You know that! Victor has lied to you!" Marvin continued to object loudly as Dan reached down and grabbed him by the hair again. This time he did not let go until the two were in the basement.

Dan had two handcuffs hanging from an oak beam crossing the basement ceiling. He had guessed Marvin to be slightly taller than he was, so once Marvin was in the cuffs with his ankles bound together, he had to stand on the tips of his toes to relieve pressure from his wrists. It looked extremely uncomfortable to Dan, which made his miscalculation a delightful surprise. Dan sat down on the sofa in front of Marvin as he listened to him pile lie upon lie. Never saying a word, while Marvin wove his story.

It was not but a few minutes, and Marvin's uncomfortable position changed his demeanor and he switched from his story telling to lecturing. He was hurting and desperately wanted to be taken down from the cuffs, but Dan continued to simply sit and stare blankly at him.

"God damn it, Daniel! Get me down from here! Don't you know who I am? You'll be executed for this if you don't stop this madness, NOW!"

Fifteen minutes passed before Dan arose from the chair. He walked to the corner of the room and found a small box for Marvin to stand on.

"There. Now, let's talk, Marvin. The photo is real, Marvin. You did unspeakable evil to my precious baby girl, Marvin. You caused the death of my wife, Marvin, and you turned me into a monster. But, before we get your confession, I'm going to give you mine. You see, Marvin, you will not be the first devil I have killed. No, no, no. Not by a long shot. I've been doing this to monsters like you for years, and I have perfected my art."

"I'm telling you they are not real, Dan! You are going to get the needle for a lie! Don't throw your life away! Mason took your daughter! Mason killed your daughter, not me! I was never there! Victor was using that photo to blackmail me. It's a fake, I'm telling you!"

At that, Dan pulled another photo from his pocket. The one with Mason and Marvin both posing with his daughter. He held it in front of Marvin's eyes, and for a split second, Marvin appeared to be enjoying the photo. A moment later and he was back to his denial.

"Marvin, I'm going to be honest with you. I have murdered 98 pedophiles over the last 17 years, and you have not said one thing that I have not already heard a dozen times. They were all innocent, or framed, or just good men who had been mischaracterized and mistreated. They all began with those very same lies, Marvin. You know what else they all did? Do you? They all admitted their guilt in the end, and so will you. The end will not come until you have, so I hope you drag this out as long as possible. I want you to suffer, oh I do, but you will look me in the eye and admit what you did to my daughter. You will, or the hell you have just entered will not end."

Dan pulled a small knife from his pocket as Marvin began screaming with all his energy. He held the knife to Marvin's throat for a moment before cutting the shirt from him. Dan continued, while Marvin screamed continuously, until he had removed every article of clothing from his captive. With Marvin standing nude in front of him, Dan kicked the box from under him and left him to hang there while he set up his video equipment. He not only wanted to hear his confession, but he wanted the world to hear what a US Senator had done to his 8-year-old daughter. Dan wanted there to be no doubt in anyone's mind that what was about to happen to Marvin was done for a reason.

"Hello, my name is Daniel Stoker, and this recording will bear witness to the confession and punishment of the man who took everything from me. The man behind me is a man not worthy of living. In fact, he is no man at all but a demon. Behind me is

US Senator Marvin Langford, and before this video ends, he is going to explain to you what he did to my daughter. I warn you, this video will be graphic, but necessary all the same. This is my daughter. This photo was taken less than an hour before Marvin's son Mason abducted my baby. She was only 8-years-old." Dan began to cry a little as he held the four black and white photos taken of him and his daughter in front of the camera.

"This is Marvin Langford posing with the corpse of my baby girl two days later." The tears began to flow a little more as he held up the polaroid for the camera. "He has denied any involvement despite the photos I have in my possession, but we will soon learn the truth. This bloody fingerprint on the edge of this photo belongs to Mr. Langford. The blood belongs to my daughter. I know this, and DNA analysis will confirm it. He continues to lie, but I swear, the lies will all end soon."

He took his seat on the sofa once again and quietly watched Marvin as he continued to profess his innocence and beg for help. Five minutes or so had passed before Dan returned to Marvin.

"You had your chance to confess. You refused, so now I will extract it from you, Marvin, and I am very good at doing so and will enjoy it very much. This is going to be very painful Marvin. Thank you!" Dan whispered into Marvin's ear as he stood in front of him.

Dan went back to the sofa and began searching through a large duffel bag he had brought with him. Moments later he returned to Marvin with a 6-inch hunting knife and a small butane torch. Upon seeing the two items, Marvin nearly fainted, for he knew their purpose. Dan would start with what he promised to do to Becky's killer all those years ago.

Dan lowered the knife between the legs of Marvin and looked coldly into his eyes before slicing the blade into his flesh. With several firm slashes, Dan removed any chance of Marvin ever raping another child. It was bloodier than he had imagined, but the butane torch soon cauterized the wound. Marvin's screams could be heard halfway down the drive, though there was no one around to hear him.

Dan held up the amputated appendage for Marvin to see, but he refused to open his eyes.

"Open your fucking eyes or I'll cut your fucking eyelids off, Marvin!" Dan screamed in his face as he grabbed him by the back of the head.

Marvin was groaning in agony as he reluctantly opened his eyes.

"Oh, God…" Marvin vomited on himself before briefly passing out at the sight of himself in Dan's hand.

Dan returned to the sofa and patiently waited for Marvin to awake. He scanned the room, noticing for the first time in the corner a very old brass scale, or rather set of scales all hanging from an intricately decorated walnut post. It was a Bavarian Pharmacy Balance used in the 19th century to allow the pharmacist to precisely compound patient's medications. At the base of the post were four small brass supports positioned 90 degrees from one another, each in the shape of an expertly crafted dragon's head. At the top, were four brass arms shaped as long curving leaves, from which the scales hung. The scales were of varying sizes for measuring a variety of weights, and each pan was a work of art in itself. Some were made from bone, others from porcelain, and all formed perfectly by hand. Dan made his way to the corner and stood there admiring the old but extremely accurate instrument. He thought it fitting that such an instrument be present as the scales of justice were brought upon Marvin.

A few minutes passed and Marvin began to come to, so Dan stood and returned to his captive. Dan grabbed him by his wrinkled and sagging throat as he told Marvin his fingers would be next. To demonstrate, Dan lopped off his left pinky finger with a pair of cable cutters, then cauterized the wound with his butane torch. He followed that with a punch to the ribcage of Marvin, which clearly fractured bone. Marvin wailed loudly then began begging Dan to kill him. The pain he was in was unbearable, and Marvin had come to the realization that his suffering would only end in his death. He could no longer stand, and the cuffs were cutting into his wrists from the weight of his body.

"Confess and I will release you." Dan whispered in his ear as he lopped off a second finger.

Marvin's head dropped low as he agreed. As Marvin spoke, Dan was overcome with the pain of remembering that day. Marvin spoke with such clarity and detail that one would have thought the murder had taken place yesterday, not 19 years prior. As he told the story, Dan sat on the sofa sobbing quietly with his head in his hands. As the story unfolded, Marvin's tone changed, as if he was enjoying remembering it. He confessed to the rape and murder of Becky, to molesting Mason for years and for murdering him to conceal their crime. He confessed to the enjoyment he received from seeing Dan so tormented, and yet so thankful to him. He said it was true power.

Dan's head raised from his hands as he realized Marvin was actually enjoying the retelling of his daughter's murder. He looked on in disgust as he continued with the details, until Marvin paused and looked at Dan with a cruel smile.

"She was such a pretty little thing."

Dan punched Marvin again in the side, this time so hard he broke several ribs in two. Marvin, in agony, let out another round of high-pitched screams as Dan continued to pound on his torso. Dan punched until he was exhausted, and it wasn't until then that he realized Marvin was on the verge of death.

Dan recited Luke 17:2 to Marvin as he removed the small folding knife from his pocket. He pressed the blade inside one of the nostrils of Marvin's nose as he explained the meaning of the verse. Doubtlessly, Marvin would have much rather drown than suffer the slow and painful death he was experiencing. Dan sliced the nostril open with the knife blade, then began carving "Luke 17:2" across the forehead of Marvin.

Agent Jennings had just made it to the top of the stairs when she heard the unhinging screams of Marvin. She paused for a moment to listen, as at first the sounds did not sound human. It was not until she heard Marvin's voice begging to die that she shattered the stained glass and opened the door. With gun in hand, she cautiously stepped through the doorway and called for Dan.

"Mr. Stoker, this is Special Agent Casey Jennings. Are you in here?"

Though crumpled up on the floor and barely conscious, Marvin managed to screech out one last call for help before Dan wrapped the tourniquet around his neck. Dan knew he was caught, but he did not care. The only thing that mattered was to finish Marvin. Finish him, and Dan's work would be done. Agent Jennings was too late. She could not stop it. Dan would not allow her to stop him. Halfway through Marvin's plea for help, Dan cinched the rope down tight on his neck and lifted him up off the ground with both hands.

Marvin's face was purple, and his body was thrashing about wildly as Agent Jennings descended the stairs towards the basement. She could hear the commotion but proceeded slowly and cautiously with her gun drawn. The sight that awaited her was as gruesome as she had ever seen. As she made it to the base of the staircase and rounded the corner, she was met with one of the most horrifying crime scenes she had ever witnessed. Dried blood everywhere from Dan's time with Victor, as well as two men, both covered in blood and one naked, standing not 20 feet from her. Marvin's face was a deep purple, and his eyes blood red, his body still twitching back and forth as he clung to life. Dan standing behind him with the tourniquet handle slightly above his head. Marvin was easily a foot off the ground as Dan gripped the wooden dowel tight. He was looking at Agent Jennings with utter defiance on his face as she attempted to gain control of the situation.

"Let him go, Mr. Stoker! Let him go now! I will not let you kill this man!" She shouted across the room.

Hearing those words only further fueled Dan's rage. Nothing would stop him, especially her. The veins in his neck bulged as he grunted and extended his arms above his head. By then, Marvin had quit twitching and Agent Jennings was forced to act. She fired two shots from her 9mm into the side of Dan, right at the base of his ribcage. The impact of the bullets stunned Dan enough for him to drop his arms to his side momentarily, but he recovered almost instantly and lifted Marvin off the floor again. This time he turned so that Marvin was in-between him and Casey, as to shield him from further fire.

It was then that Casey realized just how terrible an act Dan had committed. She recognized Senator Langford about the same time she realized Dan had removed his genitalia. She gagged at the sight, and shouted one last warning to Dan, though he remained defiant. In a swift motion, she lunged to her left and fired once more, this time striking Dan squarely in the chest. He held Marvin for a second or so longer before dropping him and falling back against the wall and slumping to the floor. His breathing was ragged, and Agent Jennings could hear the blood gurgling from across the room.

She rushed to Senator Langford's side and hastily unwrapped the tourniquet from his neck with one hand while she trained her gun on Dan with the other. She was checking for a pulse when Dan muttered between breaths.

"Is...he...dead."

She did not answer, but the look on Agent Jennings face told Dan that his work was complete. He slowly reached his hand up to his shirt pocket and removed the polaroid of Marvin with his Becky and tossed it to Casey. His breaths were growing weaker by the second, and Dan knew that he would be dead within minutes. He again reached into his shirt pocket, this time removing the four black and white photos of him and Becky, as well as the unopened pack of cigarettes he had purchased the day of her disappearance.

He fumbled helplessly with the wrapper until Agent Jennings mercifully came and assisted him. She unwrapped the package and removed a cigarette as she questioned Dan.

"Why, Mr. Stoker? What have you done?"

As Dan struggled to inhale the lit cigarette, he handed the four tiny photos to Casey. It was then that she realized the girl in the photo with Senator Langford was Dan's daughter. A bit of sympathy for Dan overcame her as a tear rolled from her eye and down her cheek.

"I'm sorry Mr. Stoker, I truly am. I'll see to it the truth is told."

Dan gasped for breath as he struggled to speak.

"The...truth...is...in...my...barn...I...too...am a...monster."

Agent Jennings was considering the meaning to his statement as Dan exhaled one final drag from his cigarette. The light was fading from his eyes, as he closed them one last time and thought only of his two girls. With his last thoughts he asked for forgiveness once more and prayed to see his Becky and Shelly again. Agent Jennings took the cigarette from Dan and pressed it out against the floor. She sat down on the sofa and cried as she continued to question the meaning of Dan's last words.

Dan was gone, and Agent Jennings was left with two dead men and a lot of unanswered questions. Her answers awaited her in Oklahoma.

Chapter 14

Finding the Answers

A return trip to Oklahoma would have to wait for a day. Casey had drove through the night to catch up with Dan and was in desperate need of rest. After local law enforcement had secured the scene, Casey found a hotel in Lexington and slept until early that evening. When she woke, Casey immediately began researching Victor Berghoff and any connection he might have had with Marvin Langford.

Victor's body was not at the crime scene, but from the amount of dried blood in the basement, Casey believed that Dan had executed him days earlier. It was there in the hotel room in Lexington, KY that Agent Jennings began to understand that Daniel Stoker might have uncovered a pedophile ring of wealthy aristocrats. She spent the remainder of the night investigating, and soon found the connection she had suspected. Victor Berghoff, a known sexual deviant, had business ties with her missing William Beckmann. Could it have been that William and Victor were both involved in Rebecca Stoker's death? Had Daniel discovered their complicity and executed all involved? If so, there were bound to be more bodies.

"Is that what you meant, Daniel? Are their bodies in your barn?" She slammed her laptop closed and began packing her things. She could wait no longer. All the answers Casey needed were back at Dan's farm in west Oklahoma, and she wasted no time getting there.

Casey was rumbling over the cattle guard at the entrance to Dan's farm an hour after sunrise a day and a half later. When she stepped from her vehicle, she could not help but notice how beautiful the day was. It was warm, and bright, and the wind carried the scent of wildflowers through the air. She stretched her arms and breathed deeply as she took it all in.

She could see the roof of the barn in the skyline behind the house. Seeing it gave Casey a slight nervousness. She fully expected to find the bodies of both Victor and William inside the barn, but also considered the possibility of finding even more. Could Dan have had a longer list of men he held responsible for Rebecca? She was nervous, but also somewhat excited to learn the truth Dan had spoken of.

The sight that met Casey as she rounded the corner of the house and entered the backyard was surprising, and mesmerizing. So much so, she forgot for a moment why she was there and veered from the barn. Rebecca's Garden was in full bloom, and it was one of the prettiest places Casey had ever laid eyes on. She paused for a moment at the entrance to read the words in the wrought iron archway.

"Rebecca's Garden...Daniel, it's beautiful." Casey strolled down the covered walkways admiring Dan's work. He had poured his heart and soul into the garden, and it showed. The blooms from the dogwoods were falling to the ground and blanketing the walkways with their white petals. Flowers of all kinds lined each walkway, providing a sea of color under the branches cloaked in white.

Casey had nearly made it to the back of the garden when she spotted the first metal tag hanging from one of the dogwoods. She took it in her hand and read the words engraved upon it.

"It were better for him that a millstone were hanged about his neck, and he cast into the sea, than that he should offend one of these little ones. Luke 17:2 Hmmm." She did not understand the significance of the tag until she flipped it over and read the other side.

"Lane Christopher. #9. What? Why?"

Casey was lost for words and utterly confused. Why would Lane's name be hanging from a tree in the middle of Nowhere, Oklahoma. Seeing the name sent chills down her spine as she was forced to remember a name that she had forgotten so long ago. Lane Christopher had been a foster parent of Casey's for the better part of a year when she was eleven, and he was anything but a good man. He was one of those who had put her through hell. An abuser, molester, and drug addict who had fooled everyone in the system. Casey had never spoken a word of her abuse to anyone, and to her knowledge Lane had never been arrested for such crimes. He had to be close to 70-years old by then, and she had assumed him to be dead from the years of alcohol and street drugs. Why was his name on that tree?

187

It was then that Casey noticed the large circular grass covered mound between her and the trunk of the tree. She studied it for a moment, then looked around her and saw that all the trees had the same, almost perfectly round mound under it. It was not big enough for a grave, so Casey was lost as to what they were. She walked to the next tree in the row, and it too had the same tag, with the same verse, but with a different name. That one she did not recognize. Casey went from tree to tree, row to row, checking each tag, and they all were the same. One side, Luke 17:2, and the other side, a name, a number, and a date.

Three other names Casey recognized from past cases investigated by the FBI. All three were known pedophiles.

"Were they all pedophiles? Did Daniel kill all those men?" Casey pondered those questions in her mind as she rounded the corner to the final row in the garden.

It was not until Casey had reached #97 that her questions were answered.

"William Beckmann, #97. #97. Oh my God…he did kill all these men!!" In front of the tree was the same size mound, only this one had but a small amount of new grass growing from it, as if it had been dug recently. Casey rushed to the next tree to discover Victor's name, #98, and a mound of fresh dirt beneath it. Casey fell to the ground and sat as she looked around the garden in both disgust, and admiration. She did not condone Dan's actions, but at the same time thought those men surely deserved to die.

She walked to the next tree and found the name she assumed would be there. Marvin Langford, #99, though unlike the others, there was no mound beneath it. Casey saw that there was but one tree left and approached it somewhat cautiously as she speculated on who's name would be on the tag.

"Daniel Stoker, #100. You knew you were going to die." Casey was shocked to find the tag dated two days prior, but with a different verse on the backside.

"Lord, hear my voice: let thine ears be attentive to the voice of my supplications. Psalms 130:2"

It was Dan's last appeal to God for mercy. Casey began crying as she read the tag. Dan was a murderous man, but she somehow had pity, and even understanding for him. After all, he had killed one of the men she had wished to kill herself so many years ago. If they were all as evil as him, she could not help but understand. Casey left Rebecca's Garden as tears streaked down her face and headed to the barn.

"The truth is in my barn. What have you got in there Daniel?" She wiped the tears from her face with the sleeve of her shirt as she entered the barn.

Inside the barn was nothing of significance. Casey wandered the large, dimly lit room and searched for what Dan had called the truth. All she found was perfectly organized tools and equipment that seemed to have no connection whatsoever to the murders. At the front of the barn, she noticed the door leading to Dan's apartment. It was locked, but after a few stiff kicks, it gave way, and Casey stepped inside.

When she flipped the light on, she noticed it immediately. The thick, worn journal conspicuously placed at the center of the bed. She took it from the bed and sat in Dan's chair in front of the fireplace as she scrolled through the pages. Casey had found the truth Dan spoke of.

Each murder was horrifically detailed, each one from 1 to 98. It was not only an account of each murder, but also an insight as to why he selected each man, and why he thought death was a fitting punishment.

On the final page, Dan confessed to the sins contained in the journal, and explained why he was no better than any of his victims, why he too deserved death. Of them all, he considered the worst of his sins to have been failing to protect his family. A final plea of mercy from God filled the last paragraph, and he ended the book with one simple request of the reader:

"…bury me in Rebecca's Garden."

www.ingramcontent.com/pod-product-compliance
Lightning Source LLC
Chambersburg PA
CBHW020120180626
46812CB00006B/2671